MERLIN'S SECRET

P J SEYMOUR

MERLIN'S SECRET

P J SEYMOUR

Book One of a Merlin pair

JJ
JayJec

MERLIN'S SECRET

JayJec is the self-publishing brand for P J Smithyman. For queries regarding rights, contact: jayjec.create@gmail.com

ISBN 978-1-7394125-2-4

This edition: February 2024

To my precious Mum
For keeping the faith even when I'd lost mine!

Table of Contents

TOR MERLINUS

'Augustus, my friend, wake up!'

Huddled in a deep mossy hollow covered with leaves, Augustus did not want to wake up. He stirred in his sleep and turned over.

'AUGUSTUS!'

The old mouse opened one eye, blinked and opened the other. His ears pricked up and his nose twitched. He sighed.

'Come, my servant, I have great need of thee,' said the same voice more gently.

Augustus rolled onto his paws and shook his coat. 'Is it thee, Sire? Merlin?' he croaked.

'Indeed! Come out of thy nest to parley.'

Augustus crawled out of his shelter and looked around. A flat-sided rock rose up beside him, like a cliff. He sniffed the chilly breeze. It brought a medley of stories that floated on the air and his whiskers twitched. Sadly, it seemed there was no time to check them out.

'I have a task for thee and 'twill be a great adventure,' the voice rumbled. 'Listen carefully for there is little time to lose and much danger. Ye are to go to London and meet there the new King. I must give him the greatest secret of all – the secret of good kingship. The journey will be hard but I will protect thee on thy way. Go to where he sleeps at Buckingham Palace. His spirit must travel by dream. Bring it to me with these words:

> *'Sleep the sleep of quiet minds*
> *For when these Isles may find they need*
> *A Leader, strong in word and deed.*
> *Come then to me, who's always there:*
> *A guide, a seer,*
> *Who does not fear*
> *A future dark! For I can sing*
> *The Song of Old that gives men heart*
> *And tell thee how to play thy part.'*

'But, Sire, there is no secret in these words!'

Augustus heard a deep chuckle. 'Aye, mice do not sing, they cannot know what this means, so thou art the safest messenger of all. When I have the spirit of the new King before me, then, my trusty servant, ye shall understand.'

'Sire,' pleaded Augustus, 'I am old and afeard. Thus was my daughter sent long ago – the same mission exactly! She did not return. Surely, there is a better servant for thy purpose? I know not this London, nor the way of people who live there, nor the image of this King their new leader, nor the place where he sleeps, nor . . .'

'Augustus, do as I bid! Did I not give you immortality when I still lived? 'Twas for this purpose! I am Merlin, thy liege lord. My power works only through living creatures. As I have told thee before, humans must be shielded from my power. A spirit from your world that comes before me in human form is cursed for eternity. I speak to them only in other form – a bird, an animal, a reptile. It is fitting that my wisest and best servant should do such a great task. I will be with thee and there will be others to help. Come, look at the stone for I wish to show thee what to seek.'

Shadows appeared on the surface of the rock beside the mouse's cave. Slowly they shifted to form the picture of a man's face. Augustus gasped.

'See the face of the King thou must find. Now, see the place where he lies to sleep.' A second image flickered onto the stone and faded. 'Go, now, and follow the path to the place below where the people live. There, ye can rest and I shall help thee find a way to reach London.'

The hair down Augustus's back stood on end. 'Sire,' he began in a quivering voice, 'I beg thee to take away my immortality! I no longer wish to live. Truly, I am ready to leave this earth in the way of all mice. Thy mission is beyond me. Let me die and join the world of the spirit for I am ready.' Augustus gulped.

'Nay, my trusty servant, have faith. All will be well. After this task I will seek ye out and then ye shall find thy just reward.'

Augustus cast a longing glance back at his cosy hollow. 'If it is thy wish, Sire, then I will go.' With a heavy heart, he rustled through the wild grasses and jumped from rock to stone. The slope of the tor was steep and some way from the nearest village. As he struggled Augustus had time to think. Although I love Merlin, he thought, sometimes his service is a curse. I'm old and my body aches. My life has seen too much change and I want no more adventures. I will do this task for him but I am not sorry for what I said.

It was a long trek for the field mouse and he stopped to rest several times. He passed the houses on the edge of the small town and soon found himself in a street. Previous visits had never been for long but at least he knew his way around. Merlin's work was often risky for a mouse but never as scary as this.

A waft of air brought an interesting smell. Augustus sniffed and followed its direction. An empty can lay tucked against the corner of a house. He sniffed around it and found it clean enough inside. Perfect, thought Augustus, I need to catch up on my sleep. A quick nap and I'll be ready for anything in the day.

He curled up with his nose tucked under his tail and fell asleep. His dreams were strange with a lot of odd sounds: the scuff of human feet walking and running, people talking, whistles shrieking, the hiss and two-tone horn of trains, and from time-to-time a gentle rocking motion that was quite soothing . . .

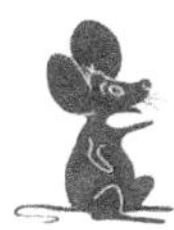

COVENT GARDEN, LONDON

Drury ran for his life. He risked a frantic glance behind him, but could not see in the street's dull lighting. His mouth dry, his heart fluttering, he raced on. He struggled with the slope of the street, his legs slowed and his breath came harder and harder.

A crisp packet flapped past him and an empty plastic bottle rolled towards him. He dodged in alarm and stopped to listen. A sheet of newspaper lifted suddenly in the breeze and floated into him. He thrashed about to shake it off. When it lifted away the pre-dawn air was hushed, as if listening with him. Then, he heard it: the faint echo of one mouse calling to another. Pete the Creep and Tony Baloney, and they were getting closer.

From the left a cat yowled; it was not far away. Panic speared his stomach. It was time to break the rules. Drury raced straight towards an Underground station – outlawed for street mice. They would never dare follow.

Drury sprinted up James Street pavement and turned into Covent Garden Underground station. The tiled flooring was slippery. Scurrying desperately under a turnstile, he turned a corner and hesitated opposite a lift. Its doors were open and its bright empty space looked welcome. A quick dash and seconds later, the doors slammed behind him.

Shaking with relief, Drury moved up against the wall and sat, panting. The lift lights hurt his eyes after the dark streets. Why can Pete and Tony steal my food, he thought, and all hell breaks loose when I lift a bit of theirs? 'Kill you,' they say. Huh. Fair exchange, I call it! Pete and Tony are forage crooks, themselves. They know the rules. They're over-reacting. It's my *territory* they really want! Well, I can play that game, too. If I can lead them astray here then double back, I can take their hunting ground. That'll teach them! All I need to do is keep calm.

The lift floor trembled slightly and jolted. Its doors opened onto a passage. Cautiously Drury peered out as a man clumped in. A tentative sniff gave no hint of danger, only a strong smell of dust, polish and stale air. He darted out. In the seconds it took to get his bearings, the doors behind him closed with a chorus of beeps. There was no going back.

Drury shuddered and moved left up the passage keeping against the wall. From the time they were weaned, every street mouse was warned about this place. It was a dangerous underworld belonging to a different tribe. The rumour was they had strange rules and savage punishments. No street mouse banished here ever came back.

He cautiously turned the corner at the end and crept down the stairs. At the bottom he turned right and darted towards the black surface of a train platform. When he peered around the wall he could see it stretched out for some distance. It felt smooth and cool beneath him. In the Opera House most of the surfaces were carpeted. Running around there was not as easy as this stuff, although it was quieter. Well, that's a good sign, he thought, cheering up. A black smooth surface and no humans: just what Dr Health-and-Safety ordered!

Drury waited keeping close to the wall, and still breathing hard. He was in a long straight hallway, which was bright as daylight but quiet and eerie. Suddenly the silence was shattered Footsteps clattered down the steps and human voices approached. He needed to hide. He ran along the wall and crouched beneath a set of metal seats. Human greetings to mice varied and one of them – a scream – gave Drury earache. They also used a lot of scary feet thumping and arm waving. No, it was a bore, so best to keep out of their way.

Glancing back towards the lifts the tiny mouse froze. Along with the humans, he could see his two pursuers. They were skulking along the wall. Oh, great: Pete and Tony still looking for revenge. A thrill of alarm raised the fur on Drury's back.

Under his paws the ground shook slightly and a distant growling noise was growing. On the streets this would mean a delivery van or truck was coming. He looked around for an escape but there was no way out. Drury heard a two-toned beeper ring out. A loud voice echoed, 'the train approaching this platform is for Heathrow. Please stand behind the yellow line.' He backed up against the wall.

A puff of wind blew back his whiskers and the fur of his coat. Suddenly, a 'poof' thumped the air. The longest noisiest machine Drury had ever seen rushed past him. Around the hall, a clicking roar boomeranged and the air blew hard along the ground. Drury heard plastic cups, pieces of card, crisp packets tumbling and snapping along the rails below. It was obviously man-made, but it had no wheels – was it a monster? Gazing up at a band of flashing lights Drury was dazed. For a moment, he felt faint at the sight. Terrified, he shuddered and shut his eyes. The rumours were true: this was a nightmare of a place.

'Oh, Merlin, help me,' he prayed, tucking his nose and eyes under a leg.

The moving lights slowed gradually, turned into windows and stopped. The machine came to rest with a screech. Watching from his hideaway, Drury saw it open its doors – lots of them – and out stepped three people who started walking along the platform. The people from the lift stepped into the brightly lit openings. The machine sat, waiting for something to happen.

Drury smoothed his whiskers back. Hm, must be some kind of bus, he realised. If humans are happy to walk into that thing, it must be okay.

Worried that Tony and Pete might pick up his trail, Drury cautiously peered down the platform. He finally spotted the two mice. They had backed up against the wall to avoid the passengers walking to the lift.

Drury waited until he heard beeping and saw the doors starting to close. Drawing his deepest breath, he streaked across the platform. As he reached the gap he launched himself towards the narrowing light. Leaping the space between platform and carriage seemed to last forever. He landed with a skid; the doors thudded together behind him. With a whine, the floor vibrated. Drury staggered across to crouch against a seat panel. He gulped for air as the floor settled into a rocking motion.

'Did it, you useless rat-snacks! Drury, you're a genius!' he gloated in relief. 'Not safe yet, but I've got away from them! It's all a question of timing, now.' He grinned to himself.

After a few minutes, the train's rocking movements slowed and it drew to a stop. 'This station is Leicester Square, change here for the Northern line,' said the train, in a human voice.

Sensing this could be a chance to escape, Drury hunched up ready to jump. When the doors slid open he hurled himself onto the platform. He scrabbled to crouch at the bottom of the wall. One mistimed move or hesitation and he would be dead. Use all your senses, he thought. There's no way Pete and Tony have kept up with me. They haven't got the nerve.

Drury found himself in a space almost exactly like the one he had left. He could see a long platform stretching out on either side of him with a domed roof far above. Along the track wall there were brightly coloured images. Peering up the platform wall next to him he could see at the top a band of tiles with a dark blue pattern like film sprockets. There was nowhere to hide.

Beside him the train closed its doors and slowly pulled away from the platform. In the quiet of its wake, Drury had an idea. He ran to the platform edge and dropped down to the track ledge. That is when he saw them. Still as lumps of coal, three mice were waiting.

Uh oh, Drury thought, here we go again.

This time Drury realized there was no way he could escape. The locals were no bigger than him, but they outnumbered him – and this was their territory. Time, perhaps, for bluffing tactics. Sitting up, Drury stroked his whiskers casually.

'Hi!' he squeaked dryly, lifting his nose in a friendly salute.

There was no reaction.

'Well, cheerio, then,' he chirruped. 'I'll leave you to it.'

'Oh no you won't,' signed one of the mice with his whiskers. Another jumped up to the platform and seconds later flopped down behind him. The two on the ledge moved forward in a businesslike way. 'You're coming with us on a nice long run through that tunnel. Don't try to escape because that would be really stupid. And stupid, here, is like . . . dead!'

NEW WORLD, NEW RULES

The Underground train carriage opened its doors. 'Out!' said Augustus's guard. He tossed his nose in the direction of the platform.

Oh, good, thought Augustus, some fresh air, at last! He stuck his head out of the carriage to check for people. There was a gap between the carriage and the platform. Should he drop through it? His guard nipped his bum so he risked a jump to the platform. No sooner had the guard leapt out to join him than the train doors closed. The train moved slowly away.

Augustus sniffed the air but his guard had no time for niceties. 'Over here,' he commanded, jabbing his snout across the platform. 'Follow and keep up or you'll get lost! Not all mice are this kind!' Dodging behind girders and columns along the platform, the guard took Augustus straight to a wall of brown tiles. He found that it surrounded the entrance to stairs going down. At a fast pace his guard led the old mouse along a sloping corridor, down a stationary escalator and up a set of steps. Reaching a platform he pattered half way along. There, he wriggled through a mesh gate into a dark recess.

'I must say you are exceedingly rude!' panted Augustus when he arrived. 'I am a visitor here on Merlin's business. All I ask for is a little help. So far, I have met with nothing but kindness. Since I arrived in London I've been treated like a criminal. Nothing to eat, nothing to drink, nothing but rudeness! You're a disgrace to the mouse community!'

'Aye, that's right, Granddad, it's tough here, right enough. You should go tell the humans,' the guard jeered, 'they might help you! But, then again, they might treat you like they treat us – a boot on the head! You keep quiet now and wait. Someone'll be along to sort you out.'

Augustus sat fuming. The two mice had not been there for long when another mouse joined them. Like the guard, his coat was black but one ear was nicked in a different pattern. He had a pleasing head, large ears, solemn eyes and a long body. He also had a confident manner. Augustus noted a few scars on his coat – he could take care of himself in a fight.

'Password!' said Augustus's guard to the new arrival.

'*Shillelagh*,' said the stranger. To Augustus it sounded like shill-ay-lee.

'Ours?'

'*Compass.*'

'Anything to report?' asked the strange mouse.

'Nothin' 'cept this,' Augustus's guard pointed his nose at Augustus. 'Another ijut outrailer! We picked him up at

Paddington. Hope you can make sense of what he's on about because we can't!'

The new mouse nodded and glanced at the cause of the trouble. He saw an old mouse with grey streaks in his dark brown coat. His muzzle was nearly white and he had no nicks in his ears. There was a calm serenity about him that was unusual. His whiskers drooped but there was a glint of humour in his bright eyes.

With a twirl of his whiskers, Augustus's guard dashed back the way he had come. Augustus realised he had been passed on. The two remaining mice eyed each other closely. 'Who are you?' asked the new mouse.

'My name is Augustus Tor Merlinus,' announced the old mouse. 'And you are . . .?'

At the mention of Merlinus, his new guard quivered and blinked. 'Merlin!' he gasped and his eyes opened wide in shock. 'I didn't know there were any of Merlin's mice left! I thought they were just a legend.'

Augustus shook his head. 'Certainly not,' he said.

The guard drew himself up and said, 'I'm Giorgio Knightsbridge, but everyone calls me Gio. I'm a Messenger of the Piccadilly line. Why are you here?'

'Merlin has given me a task. I have to take a secret to the new King who lives at a place called Buckingham Palace. Do you know the way?'

'What's a king?' asked the London mouse.

Augustus blinked. 'A man who is leader of humans, he is their chief.'

'Man?'

Augustus sighed. Not only did he have a difficult task, now he had language problems. 'A male human.'

'Phew! You've got guts, I'll say that for you!' said Gio. He thought for a moment. 'I might be able to help. Your timing's a bit off, though – curfew is starting soon. You'll have to wait and we must go somewhere safe from humans while it lasts. Come with me to the next station.'

'I need a drink,' chittered Augustus.

'Wait,' ordered Gio.

A slight tremor in the ground and a faint rumbling warned of an approaching train. It drifted into the station slowing to a squeaky halt. The two mice held back until the doors were beeping to close and then dashed aboard. Just before arriving at the next station, the train said, 'the next station is Knightsbridge. Please mind the gap.'

Gio whiskered to the old mouse, 'follow me closely.'

As soon as the carriage doors pulled apart, Gio slipped to the track ledge below the carriage instead of jumping onto the platform. Augustus found the drop deeper than he expected. He was winded when he landed on the ledge but slowly caught his breath. 'I'm sorry,' began the old mouse, 'but I must rest! I'm tired and thirsty and I simply cannot go on. All this running and jumping about is also giving me backache.'

Gio shrugged. 'This was my home station. I was born here, that's why my name is Knightsbridge. We take our first names from wall images at our birth stations. Mice have automatic rights to food and drink where they're born. Come with me, it's not far.'

He led Augustus to a set of double doors half way down the platform. They looked like metal shutters. There was a wide gap at the bottom. Behind was a storage recess with a pipe that dripped into a puddle beneath it. The water seeped slowly away through a jagged crack leading back to a small drain. Augustus sniffed at it and his lip wrinkled. 'Is it clean?' Gio nodded and took a sip. The old mouse gave in to his thirst and licked greedily from the top.

'Why are you using passwords?' asked Augustus when he was ready to talk.

Gio sat up and slowly stroked his whiskers. 'This place is a maze made by humans. They only hang around in places with lights where they wait for machines called trains. Those places we call stations and they are linked by tracks, which have no light. We find food and other stuff mainly in stations. Long ago, mouse families used to fight and feud over territory. In fact, we spent so much time and energy on warfare we nearly didn't survive.'

'I see,' said Augustus, 'go on.'

Gio glanced at him. 'Then, something strange happened. We call it the GHI – the Great Human Invasion. Humans, rats, cats, all sorts of creatures, suddenly came to live in our territory. It seems that the humans were hiding from something called, "The Jerries". We mice lived in continual curfew. It was hard to hide and even harder to find food. It was a disaster – many died of starvation.'

Augustus shook his head, as if he was hearing a story he knew well.

'Watching the humans,' continued Gio, 'we noticed they shared things and helped each other. We learned from them. When they stopped living here, we divided up the territory in the same way they did. They use different colours along each set of stations. The same trains link them up and use the same tracks. We call them lines.'

'Yes, but how did it stop the fighting?'

Gio stroked his whiskers. 'Every line has its own umpire, who is like a chief. The umpires keep order. We coordinate with other lines through meetings called Parleys. Each line has forage captains, who find food for the families on that line. Scouts do patrols or guard duty. When we're old enough one ear is nicked to show which line we belong to. Normally, we have to get permission from umpires and use a password to visit other lines. Line messengers, like me, are allowed to move about everywhere. They are trusted, so they know all the passwords.'

Nodding briefly, Augustus asked, 'does it work?'

'Yes, it does!' said Gio proudly. 'The system's been fine . . . well, until the last few years, anyway.' He paused. 'It's only the Central line that's in so much trouble.' Gio shook his coat. 'From the time I was a pup there have been odd things happening along that line. Not much at first, but it's getting worse: disappearances, killings, food shortages, too many unusual accidents and, between some stations . . . civil war. Part of my work is to find out what's going on. Sorry, it's not your problem, is it?'

'Hm, a truth-seeker!' puffed Augustus. 'I'm lucky I didn't fall into their hands. You said something about a curfew? Has it started?'

Gio nodded. 'Now, we have to wait. This is a safe place you can sleep here. Mice left this station when the humans changed it. There used to be food units on the platform and more litter on the tracks but that's all gone. We use it mainly as a meeting place now. I'll take you to the station for Buckingham Palace, but not to the streets beyond. Another tribe of mice live on the streets and we don't mix.'

'What a pity,' sighed Augustus. ' I suppose we'll have to leave it to Merlin, then.'

'Would Merlin's secret for the human chief also work for us mice?' asked Gio.

Augustus looked at him thoughtfully. 'We must find out!' he said with a half smile.

PICCADILLY CIRCUS

Boxed in by scouts, Drury ran along the tunnel. He jumped over sooty cables snaking along the floor. When trains thundered overhead on the track, he copied the other mice. They cowered low against the curved wall to wait. The wind from passing carriages blew their whiskers back and they had to flatten their ears. In such a world, Drury now understood why mice used signing so much. A twitch of whiskers, a flick of ears, a tic of the tail or the lip and, of course, the important nose; these little movements were as good as chittering or squeaking.

Near the end of the tunnel the station light threw its glow into the opening. The leading mouse slowed down and stopped to peer ahead. 'Not many humans, we should be safe enough,' he said. 'Stay in the track pit.' He led them along the central channel set deep between the tracks. Glancing up from time to time, he stopped suddenly.

'Listen,' he said.

They could all hear the faint patter of a mouse. It was hurrying along the track ledge above. Courty jumped up to see what it was. The mice below heard a gasp. 'COURTY! Oh, my goodness, am I glad to see you!' The squeak was female. A moment later Courty and a female mouse dropped to the track pit. They joined Drury and his scouts.

Generally, Drury had no time for females. He could count on *two* paws the number of times they had nearly been the death of him. In Drury's opinion, the golden formula for survival was: Female = Bad News. However, he had to admit this one looked stunning. She had a sleek body, cute whiskers, neat ears and hit-you-straight-in-the-heart eyes. But her best asset was her nose. Drury knew that male mice had preferences when it came to judging females. For some it was the eyes, for others the paws, the coat, the whiskers, the ears, but, for him, the great decider was definitely The Nose! This one was small and pointed and beautifully shaped. When she signed, it wrinkled and twitched so delicately he felt he could watch it hour after hour.

'What's up?' Courty signed to the female.

'Oh, it's Sport! He's just had his ear nicked. You know how sore it can be? Well, he's threatening to run away! I'm so worried. He's barely older than a *pup*. I think he's up to something.'

'Have you talked to his friends?'

'Of course! I asked them what was going on. They confessed they dared him to go to the Central line . . . *on his own*!' The female put her front paws to her mouth and gave a tiny mew of distress. 'I gave them all a piece of my mind and put them in detention. If any of them get onto Central line territory there'll be hell to pay!'

Courty puffed his cheeks, 'Great.'

'Please can you help? We need to tell Gio. He can warn the pups about the Central line and tell them to stay away. They're orphans, Courty! We're still teaching them the rules because they have no parents. I know Sport's naughty, but this time Gio needs to tick them all off. They won't listen to me but they think he's a hero. They'll listen to *him*.'

Drury stirred restlessly – he had also been an orphan. Her story brought back memories, none of them good. The female glanced at Courty's group. 'Oh, I'm sorry, are you busy? I can go myself.'

Drury saw his chance. He took a step forward and grinned. 'Hi, I'm Drury. I'm from the streets but I lost my way a while back. All I need is someone to show me how to get back home.' His eye twinkled at the female with practiced charm. 'We've not been introduced.' Drury looked sharply at Courty and then at the female.

Courty seemed taken aback. 'Perhaps that's because you're an outrailer not a *friend*!'

Lily stared at Drury. In that moment he felt a strange tremor in his stomach. It might have been his survival instinct warning him. More likely it was the quiver of surrender. What a star! Oh well, he thought, there's sure to be a chance to escape later. Besides, it'll give Pete and Tony time to go back and cool off.

Delicately tweaking her whiskers and twitching her nose she signed, 'I'm Lily, Lily-of-the-Valley Piccadilly Circus. To Courty she twitched, 'if you're taking him to Gio, I'm coming with you!'

Courty frowned. 'Lily, we're taking this outrailer to Gio to get rid of him, you don't need to be kind!'

Lily's mouth firmed. 'It seems to me the sooner we get to Gio the better. We're sure to find him at Knightsbridge with the curfew coming. No other lines pass through the station so we'll be safe. We don't have time to waste. Why don't we use the train?'

All the mice looked at Courty. He sighed. 'Okay, we'll take the next one.'

On his decision, the whole group leapt up to the platform edge. Drury grimly noticed his scouts stayed on each side of him. The mice scurried to hide under a metal bench but did not have long to wait. A train clicked slowly into the station and drew to a graceful halt.

'This is a Piccadilly line service to Heathrow Terminal 4 and Terminals 1, 2 and 3,' announced the station.

After waiting for any humans to get out, the mice raced across to jump into the carriage opposite. It was brightly lit so they quickly ducked beneath the seats. A loud beeping warned of the closing doors and they were on their way. As the rocking motion of the floor slowed, the train said in a human voice, 'this is Green Park. Change here for the

Victoria and Jubilee lines. Alight here for Buckingham Palace.'

Drury listened with half an ear and yawned. He noted the train gave a warning just before it stopped. Might be useful . . .

FRIENDS IN NEED

Before they could settle down for the curfew at Knightsbridge, Gio and Augustus heard a loud squeak, 'GIO!' They turned and saw a mouse wriggling under the doors. 'Lily Piccadilly Circus,' he gasped, 'what are you doing here?' The two mice greeted each other with coat sniffing and licking and they touched whiskers affectionately. Augustus watched in great interest while other mice wriggled through to join them.

'Oh, Gio, I'm so pleased to see you!' said Lily. 'Our orphan pups are driving me crazy! Little Sport wants to run away. His friends have dared him to go to the Central line *on his own*! They all need a good ticking off! Please can you come and give them a lecture about the dangers? They're at that age where they won't listen to females!'

'Sure,' said Gio, 'but I have to deal with some other stuff, first.' He gently nudged Lily to wait near Augustus. A train rumbled in to the station. It made so much noise the mice switched to signing.

'What's up, Courty?' asked Gio.

'We were checking Covent Garden for looters and we found this rat snack,' Courty pointed his nose at Drury. 'Thought we'd better bring him on to you.'

'Excuse me! Mind who you call a rat snack,' Drury retorted.

'Who are you and what are you doing here?' chipped in Gio.

'The name's Drury.' A cheeky grin appeared on Drury's face and he glanced at Lily with a smirk. 'Prince of Wales Drury Lane, if you want it in full! As for what I'm doing here, well . . . I was happily minding my own business when I was stopped by your slap tails!'

'All right, all right, no need to be insulting – *you* are invading *our* zone, in fact. Watch your manners!' Gio glared at Drury. 'You're a street mouse, aren't you?'

Drury stroked his whiskers. 'What of it?'

Gio studied him with narrowed eyes. 'Normally we have a special treatment for street mice but you may be lucky. Do you know the way to a place called Buckingham Palace?'

'Do I know it?' said Drury, 'of course, I do! Every street mouse knows that! All you have to do is take me back the way your stupid mates have come and get me to the streets. Bingo's you're uncle!'

Gio frowned. Turning to Courty he said, 'Where did you find him?'

'Leicester Square station.'

Gio snorted. 'You're a liar, Drury. Buckingham Palace isn't at Leicester Square.'

'I didn't say it was,' snapped Drury. '*We* learn a bit of human-speak when we're pups, even if you don't! The train told us where it is, didn't it?' he turned to Courty. 'Get me to that place, show me the way to the streets and your problems are over!'

Gio looked doubtful. He turned to Augustus. 'How will you know it's the right place?'

'When I see it, I will know,' rumbled the old mouse. They all looked curiously at him.

Gio told the group, 'Augustus is one of Merlin's retainers. His name is Augustus Tor Merlinus.' At the name Lily gasped. The others quivered and glanced nervously at each other. They all edged back from the old mouse and eyed him with awe.

Drury stared at the old mouse suspiciously. He sniffed and his tail twitched. 'I heard that Merlin's retainer mice had all died.'

'No, we are few, but there are still mice who serve our master.' The old mouse sat patiently, watching Drury groom his whiskers.

'Curfew has started and we must hide,' said Gio. 'Let's base up at here. Augustus can explain while we wait.'

GAME ON . . .

'Augustus, please tell us what *exactly* is your task?'

The old mouse seemed surprised. 'I thought you understood. I need to go to Buckingham Palace to give a secret from Merlin to the King who lives there. I'm not able to give any details. Only Merlin has the secret.'

Shaking his head, Gio said firmly, 'if you want us to help you, we need more than that. If we take risks on your behalf we must know more. Why now? Is it urgent? Do you know what dangers we'll face? Does the King know we're coming? How can you give him the secret if you don't know what it is?'

Augustus looked aghast. 'It's not as simple as you seem to think! No matter how I try to help you understand, there are some things you don't know. Your world is different to the countryside I come from.' The old mouse glanced round at the expectant faces before him.

'There's something else;' he hesitated, 'telling you too much could put me in danger from a powerful curse. Any mouse that breaks Merlin's rules is doomed to die with no afterlife. I believe this happened to my daughter who came to London on the same mission many years ago.'

'Go on, Gussie, don't worry about your silly ol' curse,' chipped in Drury. 'Merlin won't care. He needs us to help you!'

Augustus frowned. 'I'll tell you what I can but even I do not know all!' He sighed. 'You've probably heard mouse myths but now I'm going to tell you about the *real* Merlin. He was a wise old human who lived a long time ago, longer than you can even imagine. He was very clever and he became an adviser to the humans' leader – the King. Merlin began the habit of living in wild places. During these periods he learned much about the ways of nature. He experimented with the things he found and sometimes with creatures like us. Humans respected him for all his learning and the amazing things he could do. They called him a magician or sorcerer.

'When Merlin became old, he collected certain mice he found while wandering the countryside. He treated them well, gave them special foods to eat and liquids to drink. He talked to them as if they were humans. Gradually, Merlin and those mice learned to communicate with each other as if they were part of the same family. I think his food and drink helped the mice to learn more quickly, too – it certainly tasted very good!'

Augustus licked his lips in memory of it. The mice listening to him exchanged glances.

'To this day, the mice descended from that family are known as retainers. He marked the mice and gave them a special name: *Mus merlinus*. They lived far longer than ordinary mice and learned some of the magic he knew. Although Merlin has left his human form, he still uses his special creatures to do his bidding.'

Drury started fidgeting. 'So what?' he interrupted.

'A short time ago, Merlin spoke to me while I slept. He gave me a magic verse and told me to go to a place the humans call Buckingham Palace. There, I must recite his spell and Merlin will be able to speak with the human. He will give the new King his great and powerful secret – the secret of how to rule as a wise and strong leader. Merlin trusts only his best retainers with this task, so it is a great honour.'

Augustus looked hopefully at his audience. 'All I am asking is for help to find the way to the Palace. It is well-known to humans.'

'Fine,' snapped Drury impatiently. 'Only trouble is we happen to be *mice* and I can't see them politely showing us the way, can you?'

'You should be ashamed of yourself!' said Lily. 'Don't you *want* to help Augustus?'

Drury looked startled and his mouth opened in surprise. 'But . . . a *human*!'

Augustus intervened. 'Perhaps it was Merlin who sent Drury to guide me through the hazards ahead? I need your help Drury. You will be well rewarded by our master.'

Drury snorted in disbelief. He risked a glance at Lily's nose. 'All right, but I still think you're crazy. I'm not promising anything.'

Gio lost his patience. 'This is Merlin's business and we don't have a choice. We know what's at stake in helping Augustus. We need your skills, Drury, to help us find our way outside the station. It's not as if you'll be on your own! We're coming with him. I can promise you one thing, though: if you cause us any more trouble, it will be game over for *you*!'

Drury nodded sulkily. 'Okay, I said I'd try.' Gio flicked a disbelieving glance at Courty.

Turning to Augustus he asked, 'is there a time limit on the message?'

'As soon as may be!' The old mouse hurriedly stroked his whiskers. 'When the humans make their king! He needs Merlin's wisdom and his blessing as soon as possible. We cannot afford to dilly-dally.'

'*Dilly-dally*?' Gio sighed. 'Only a few of us can go – too many and we'll be noticed.' He looked a question at Drury's two guards. They glanced at each other and shook their heads.

One of them visibly shuddered. The other spoke for them both, 'Sorry Augustus, but there's no way I'm goin' up there an' that's final. Not ever!'

'Courty?' Gio looked at his friend hopefully.

Courty shrugged. 'Sure, I'm not afraid of a challenge.' The scornful glance he gave Drury raised the fur along the outsider's back and he frowned.

Gio looked relieved. 'Okay. Menu, when this curfew is over please go to my father. Tell him what you've heard and that I'm helping Augustus. Chutney, you better go with Lily to help her sort out the pups.'

'Forget it, Chutney,' chipped in Lily softly. 'I'm going with Gio.'

'No, you can't,' said Gio shortly. 'You're needed here to take care of the pups.'

'Oh, per-leeese . . .' began Lily.

'No, really,' insisted Gio. 'If anything happened to you, I'd never forgive myself. You're too special, Lily, and have important work to do here for the line!'

Lily's mouth grew thinner and her eyes glinted angrily as Gio spoke. 'Rubbish! Listen to me, Giorgio Knightsbridge. I'm sick and tired of hearing weak excuses about why female mice aren't strong enough, or good enough, or quick enough, to do what scouts do. Male mice keep all the exciting adventures to themselves. We're left to do the boring things you can't be bothered with. Well, I don't care, any more. I'm coming with you whether you like it or not, so you better get used to the idea!'

Gio gaped at her but Drury's eyes gleamed. 'Atta mouse!' he squeaked with a flick of his tail on the ground.

'Good, that's settled, then!' she said and went to crouch next to Augustus.

The old mouse smiled at Lily. 'Well, my dear, I couldn't wish for better companions on this mission,' he said gallantly. 'Fortune always favours the brave!'

CATASTROPHE!

As soon as the curfew was safely over the mice darted along the track pit into the station. When the eastbound train arrived, no humans stepped out. At night the station was closed. The group leapt into a carriage and the train took off with a hum. There were three passengers sitting half asleep further down.

Drury made sure he was near the doors. He glanced at Augustus hiding under a sideways seat. That old mouse is slow, clumsy and dreamy – basically, a survival hazard, he thought. Augustus must think we're stupid! Helping him is *not* going to be easy. No matter what he says he's not going to trick me into losing my life! This caper is doomed and I need to escape.

As the train slowed down, it announced sweetly, 'the next station is Hyde Park Corner. Please mind the gap.'

Drury sat up when he heard this and tensed to run. As soon as the carriage doors slid open Drury leapt out and sprinted along the platform. Courty had been watching Drury; he dashed straight after the escaping mouse. When

Gio followed, the others realised something was wrong. Menu and Chutney stayed in the carriage but the others jumped off the train. They looked quickly along the platform, saw the mice chasing each other and scampered to sit against the wall.

'Have we reached the station for Buckingham Palace?' Augustus asked Lily. 'I thought Gio told us it was Green Park station? The train said "Hyde Park Corner". Is it this Park? I'm confused!'

Lily shook her head. 'No, I think Drury has tried to escape. One thing's for sure: we can't keep up with them.' She sighed. 'We must stay with Gio. Let's wait and see.' They moved to crouch under a metal bench.

Drury flopped over the edge of the platform to run beside the track. He soon reached the dark tunnel in front of the waiting train. Without pausing, he dashed into the darkness using the train's headlight to find his way easily. At the edge of its glare he stopped to catch his breath. A whisper of sound ahead made his ears prick forward. In the faint glow from the station light he caught sight of something glimmer.

Behind him the train slammed its doors shut and started to move forward with a hum. Its headlight lit up every mouse's greatest nightmare. There in the tunnel was a scrawny tabby cat with huge green eyes. The train blinded it for a moment and it recoiled against the wall, hissing as the engine swept past. Drury froze in panic. He whirled around to retreat. Behind him, the pursuing mice also saw the cat. 'Kaiser!' gasped Gio.

Horrified, they reversed and raced back to the platform. 'Distract him,' squeaked Gio, 'I'll find Augustus!'

Drury sprinted after the two mice and was close behind when they scrabbled up the brickwork and dashed to the wall. Gio hunted frantically down the platform for Augustus and Lily. Courty darted into an exit and turned to face the approaching cat. Drury dashed past Courty down the platform to escape.

Dazed by the train, the cat hesitated in the tunnel. Head lowered, the tip of his tail twitching, Kaiser licked his lips. As the mechanical whine of the train disappeared behind him, his ears flicked forward, twitching to catch the slightest sound.

Slowly and silently, the cat paced along the track; its shoulder blades smoothly rising and falling in a stalking rhythm; it's mottled fur slipping like velvet over the hard muscles beneath. Kaiser's cold green eyes blinked steadily as he checked the scene ahead. His nose twitched as he picked up a familiar smell – mice!

As he came out of the tunnel, Kaiser hesitated. He carefully stood on his hind legs to peer over the platform edge. There were no passengers. Kaiser dropped down again to the track ledge. The smell of mouse was strong. With eyes narrowed, he leapt up onto the platform.

At one end of the east and westbound platforms is a small hallway shaped like a lace-up shoe. There are gaps on both sides to the parallel platforms with stairs and escalators at the back end like its tongue. Courty could thread the cat in-and-out of the crossover openings on the platforms. Following Gio's instructions, he zigzagged squeaking across Kaiser's path to distract the cat. Kaiser took the bait and tried to pounce but slipped on the smooth floor. Courty was too quick for him. He dodged sideways and raced for an exit to lead the cat off the platform. Kaiser followed him only to see the mouse disappear diagonally across the hallway and through the opening to the westbound platform. The cat charged across and peered around the wall. Courty waited until Kaiser came out to follow him and then sprinted to another opening back into the hallway.

The hum and vibrations that had been steadily growing in the background now peaked and a train rumbled into the station. Courty led Kaiser to the eastbound platform. By the time he returned to the opposite side the train had opened its doors. He ran a short way along the wall and waited for the cat to appear. The game of peek-a-boo was becoming too dangerous. When Kaiser's head came through the entrance, Courty dashed along the platform until the train's beeping sounded. He leapt into a carriage as it closed the doors with a slam. The train glided smoothly away.

Kaiser slowed his pace and watched his prey escape. He turned back to the other platform. This was where he had first seen the mice. He paced slowly along its length, pausing to sniff the ground. At the far end of the platform, Gio, Lily and Augustus were hiding in a passage entrance. Gio peeked around the corner of the wall. He saw the cat in the distance padding in his direction.

'Drury has gone to the tracks to hide. Come on, we must run,' he said to the others behind him.

They crossed to the westbound platform and ran along the bottom of the wall. By the time they reached the access area where Courty had dodged Kaiser, a train pulled in to the other platform. The mice crossed the stairs hallway and checked for Kaiser. He was sitting some way down the platform hiding under a bench. He caught sight of the mice but was too far to catch them. They ran across the platform and jumped aboard. Behind the cat, Drury leapt up to the platform edge. He shot a glance down the platform. Kaiser was trotting towards the other end. Drury quickly dived into the carriage next to him and hid under a seat.

The train's warning beeps flustered Kaiser and the slamming doors startled him. He veered towards the wall as the train started to pull away from the station. As the last carriage entered the tunnel, Kaiser went to the platform edge. He jumped down to the tracks and stalked after it.

GREEN PARK

Gio was in despair: had Kaiser killed Courty? It was his fault. He had asked Courty to distract Kaiser and his friend must be dead as a result. *I'm going to kill that selfish, useless, rat-hearted Drury! It's his fault for getting off the train and running away.* He thought of all the painful things he could do to punish Drury. He glanced at Augustus and Lily crouched under a nearby seat. How lucky they had been to jump on board before Kaiser could react! As he felt the train slow down, Gio forced himself to think ahead.

When the train screeched to a halt, Gio pointed his nose at the doors. 'Drop down to the track ledge,' he signed, 'and stay against the wall. I'll fetch you as soon as I can.' He jumped out and scanned the platform in both directions. Catching sight of a tail disappearing over the platform edge, Gio ran to the spot. He peered down to the track ledge and saw a mouse hurrying away under the train. He dashed along the platform and pounced from above.

'Gotcha!' screeched Gio before he bit into Drury's neck.

Drury whirled around and tried to bite him off but to no avail. Desperate to get away from the weight of his attacker, Drury pulled them both to the edge. After a strong tug, the two mice fell into the pit. Landing first, Drury was winded and could not move as he tried to catch his breath. Gio was the first to recover.

'You filthy, rotten . . .' Gio tried to think of the worst thing he could call Drury. 'RAT!' he panted. Brutally rolling Drury over with his snout, he shouted, 'Get up!'

Dazed and coughing Drury struggled up as the train overhead closed its doors and began to pull away. Staggering and panting for breath, himself, Gio chivvied Drury along the pit towards the others.

'If you try to make another run for it, Drury, I'll kill you,' he gasped. 'Why did you run off like that? You've caused Courty's death! A first class mouse: one of the best. All we want from you is help to take Augustus to his palace. If you get us there I might, *might*, let you go.' He nipped Drury on the bum and yelled, 'get up there to the ledge! Try a stunt like that again and I will definitely bump you off. I won't hesitate; it'll be a pleasure!'

Drury jumped up to find Lily and Augustus waiting. 'Yeah, yeah, yeah,' he chittered, still catching his breath. 'You don't *know* Courty's dead! You were *never* going to take me back to my station! What did you think I was going to do? Sit and watch the chance to escape pass me by? You're keeping me against my will! Green Park, Hyde Park, what's the difference? You've got no right to force me . . .'

'QUIET!' thundered Augustus like a parent with two squabbling children. He frowned severely at Drury as he spoke slowly and icily. 'As you very well know, Drury, this place seems to be the hunting ground of a feral cat! I would suggest that you delay your plans to escape until it is safe to do so. In the meantime, is this the station for Buckingham Palace?'

Gio sighed. 'Yes, it is. I'm going to take us up to the main station hall. One of the exits goes to The Green Park.' He stared meaningfully at Drury. 'That's where your street smarts come in handy.'

Drury caught Lily's eye. 'Fine,' he sulked. 'Let's go, then.'

Gio shook his head but cautiously led the group of mice to an arched opening at the end of the platform. It had a 'Way out' sign at the top. Beyond it was a lobby area, which had giant escalators slowly creeping up and down from the other side. The mice darted across. When they reached the upward escalator, Augustus dithered. A nip on his behind from Drury sent him on his way with a jump. He dropped down onto the step behind. 'What was that for?' he demanded.

'Looked like you needed help,' said Drury. 'With moving stairs all you do is watch the squares come out, choose one, hop onto it and wait. Simple.'

Augustus sniffed. 'We didn't have these when I was young but I know what to do. I may be slow but I'm not stupid. When I want help I'll ask for it!'

Drury nodded. 'Okay, but I think you need to get ready.' He pointed with his nose over Augustus's shoulder.

The escalator juddered slightly and flattened out. Augustus jumped over the metal teeth waiting to eat up the stairs at the end. He shook himself and waited for the others. As soon as they had all jumped off the escalator, the mice raced forward and stopped against a wall ahead of them.

A line of turnstiles divided the concourse with station business on the other side. The group of mice sat and stroked their whiskers as they looked around. It was a big station with cream tiled flooring. White tiled pillars of different sizes were scattered across the ticket hall. Pillars made it easier to cross open spaces unseen. Beyond the turnstiles the station seemed to stretch away even further.

Lily came across and sniffed Augustus's coat. 'Are you alright?'

Augustus smiled. 'Never better, my dear,' he signed.

'Psst,' Gio signalled to the mice to follow him. They trooped under a turnstile, waited, and then dashed across to a pillar directly ahead. They were in the second half of the concourse. Around it were a closed snack stall, staircases, doors, cupboards, and automatic ticket machines set into the wall opposite. In the distance to the left they could see a wide passageway leading out of the hall.

'Where do we go from here?' Augustus asked Gio.

'I'm not sure because there are so many exits. We have to keep moving or humans will see us. We must leave the station the easiest way we can. Follow me!'

He dashed across to a bank of ticket machines set into the opposite wall. Its black cement skirting along the bottom provided cover for the mice. A whiff of cold night air blew into the station from the distant passageway at one end. The smells it carried proved they were close to the outside world. Closely followed by the others Gio darted along the wall. Where it ended the mice faced a long gap with no cover.

Gio's whiskers twitched. He hesitated for an instant and flicked his ears around. It was quiet except for the vibration of a truck on the road overhead. Gio raced across the gap into the passageway, which sloped upwards. Behind him the group followed as best they could.

The mice emerged onto a gravel circle open to the night sky. Overhead stars gleamed like diamonds on black velvet. The moon bathed everything in a soft glow. Leaves rustled in the cool breeze. Some litter snapped as it slithered over the surface of a path and hit a railing. Branches scratched a fence post; a window banged on a building near by. Lily shivered and crept closer to Augustus. 'What's that?' she squeaked.

'Nature!' said Augustus and breathed deeply.

'So, Drury, where's the place called Buckingham Palace?' queried Gio. 'I brought us here, now it's your turn to guide us.'

Drury stared at him. 'I don't know. I'm a street mouse not a parky!'

'Great,' exploded Gio, 'So, we're lost?'

AUGUSTUS TAKES CONTROL

Shivering in the night air, Augustus realized he would need to cheer everyone up and keep the group moving. 'I'm sure we're on the right track,' he said to encourage them. 'We must have faith that Merlin is watching over us. He will show us the way. However, I suggest we leave the open sky – never safe in the country. Who knows what danger lurks above?' The others exchanged glances. Above? Sometimes old mice said strange things and sometimes they said ordinary things in strange ways. 'This human pathway goes to trees over there. We must follow it.'

Gio nodded and the mice set off. They started slowly but as they scurried along, they sniffed at their surroundings and perked up. When they reached the shelter of a line of trees, a squirrel startled them. She sat still for a moment, stared at the mice and then bounded up a nearby tree trunk.

Augustus sat up. He shocked the others when he let out a long screech at the squirrel. The little animal chittered back. Augustus squeaked loudly once again. Turning to the amazed mice he said, 'Nutty tells me we're on the right track. We must continue in this direction until we get to a signpost. It points the way to everything. There, we will see the golden mount that stands before the Palace. To reach the Palace we must cross the road. I told you Merlin would guide us, and he has!'

The mice darted along their path to an area where the trees grew dense. They came upon a black signpost, which rose up in the dimness with arms spread wide. Drawn by the sound of traffic and headlights, they peered towards an enormous gate. It stood in the middle of a low cream-coloured wall to separate the park from the road on the other side. The gate's black bars stretched far into the night sky. Gold on their tips and its crests reflected the glow of street lamps.

Through the gate the mice could see a huge floodlit edifice. It was white and there was something gold at the top. They moved towards it slowly at first and then faster. The closer they trotted; the clearer became the vision through the gate. When they reached the gate, they all sat up on their tails to stare at the splendid mound ahead of them. At the top a great creature was spreading golden wings that did not move.

Augustus broke the spell. 'Ah, the golden mount!' he exclaimed. 'It guards the Palace. This is just as Nutty told us. We must keep going,' and he moved on with new energy. Puffing for breath, Augustus came up to the edge of the road and then veered right, along a broad pavement. 'There it is,' he twittered, 'the Palace!'

As the others hurried behind him, they could see a dark grey mass rearing up ahead. It was ringed with a wall and black railings like the gate they had jumped through. A few spotlights shone up at the mass and made it easier to see. It had a rough, knobbly surface interrupted with glass squares along it's front. The closer the mice came to it, the bigger it loomed. It went on and on as far as they could see, dominating the horizon left, right and upwards.

As they scurried, a vehicle thundered towards them. Its headlights were bright, it flashed with blue and it screamed with a high-pitched wail.

'Watch out!' Gio yelled.

Augustus stopped, Gio turned to protect Lily, while Drury ran to hide behind a lamppost. It swept passed the huddle of tiny creatures bowling them over. Shuddering with fright, they cowered together beside a traffic light.

'How will we cross this space?' fretted Augustus, quivering.

'Don't worry,' soothed Lily, 'we're nearly there.'

Strangely, traffic seemed to cease in the wake of the noisy truck. Augustus glanced at the others. As if to a signal, they all dashed with tails up across the glistening mauve road. They did not stop running until they had crossed the pavement and reached the safety of a wall. Trotting along its base, Drury glanced towards the golden mount. He froze.

'Oh, my word,' he sounded breathless. 'Will you look at the size of that cat?'

All three mice snapped round to see what he was looking at. Sure enough, in the stark floodlights a giant cat was prowling alongside a human. It was enormous. The cat seemed to have frozen, as they do when they spot their prey. The mice waited in panic. As he stared at the nightmare creature, Augustus noticed there was another one on the other side of the monument. Neither cat moved at all. He blinked several times and checked. No, they did not change position even by a fraction.

He chuckled in relief. 'The cat's not alive, Drury,' he explained. 'Humans have learned the art of creating life-like images of things they worship, or admire, or simply want to remember. They call them statues. It is evidence of great fondness or value. They must have adored this cat to create such a large statue. Come, we must move on.'

Reassured but still puzzled, the mice came to a gate of railings. They trotted under it to shelter behind a stone gatepost. In the glare of lights, the façade rising up before them made their project seem more daunting.

'Now what?' asked Drury, panting.

TRESPASSERS

Augustus sat up and studied the panorama stretched out before him. There were three entrances with arched gates at the bottom of the building. Two pillbox guardhouses with a pointed roof stood on each side.

'I think we should try one of the smaller entries.' murmured Augustus. He pointed with his nose towards the arched gateway nearest the mice.

The others agreed so they set off. The mice sprinted and paused, like human commandos, to the building ahead. Slithering through a gap along the bottom of the gate, they found themselves in a giant quadrangle. In the centre of the opposite side a screen of frosted glass stretched between stone pillars. Above it was a second layer of columns and on top of that an ornate carved triangle of stone. Silence reigned.

They sprinted to one side of the glass screen and from there they spied a stairway. The door at the top was closed. After scampering up the steps, the mice found a gap wide enough to slip into the room behind. They paused inside the threshold to decide which way to go. Stretching out before them was a sea of red carpet. The white ceiling with its intricate gilding reflected moonlight from the windows. Moonlight glinted on gilt niches in the corners of the room and on the staircase to the left. Huge floral bouquets were scattered around the big hall, which did not have much furniture.

The mice sniffed the air to check for hazards. There were no people. Gio darted cautiously across the carpet to the centre of the room to look for an exit. He gasped as he caught sight of the Grand Staircase. An Everest of red carpet rose higher and higher and, unlike the escalators at home, these steps did not move. The others joined him. 'I think the only way is up there,' he said.

Augustus sighed. He was worried about his back. 'I agree, we must go up, as Gio says.'

'Keep to the soft stuff,' warned Gio.

They set off again, leaping up the steps until they reached the second landing. Here they rested to wait for Augustus. On the landing at the top of the stairs, the mice paused beside a plinth below a small statue. A doorway on the right led into an anteroom with some white marble statues so they ambled in. The human statues seemed very lifelike in the shadowy light. At first, the group of mice froze, but the statues did not move. Timidly, Augustus moved a pace. He sniffed up at a dog leaning against his mistress's leg. The dog did not move and he did not smell like animals in the country. Must be one of those statues, he thought and moved on cautiously.

Moonlight shone through the massive windows down one side of the next room. The mice could make out a scattering of gilt furniture and dark images framed also in gilt on the green walls. Huge chandeliers hanging from the ceiling twinkled with millions of fiery sparks to brighten up the darkness.

Augustus made for the doors ahead. There, the group found themselves in the doorway of a vast hall. It was lit from moonlight streaming in down one side and glimmering off massive chandeliers above. A lighter mottled carpet made the area seem brighter and bigger. Strangely, there was no furniture: nowhere to hide. The group hesitated.

'Look, Augustus, this is starting to get scary. What exactly are we looking for?' asked Drury.

'We're not there, yet,' said Augustus calmly. 'I must deliver my secret to one special human – there can be no others present, you understand? Merlin has advised that the magic works when the King is asleep. So we must find his nesting place. This is a palace – there are many possibilities. I sense we're getting closer but we must hurry.'

Drury clicked his tongue. 'Oh, is that all? Come off it, Augustus,' he exploded. 'We could spend *the rest of our lives* in this place hunting for it!'

Augustus ignored him. Conscious of the time, he took the plunge and trotted confidently up the centre. His companions spread out cautiously, scampering after him. Augustus seemed to know what he was doing. He found an exit and dashed into the next room quickly. It felt familiar somehow. Glancing along to the left he thought it looked rather like a station platform. Moonlight shone through the skylight overhead casting a pearly glow everywhere. Posters in frames lined the walls and the wooden floor gleamed in the same way.

'Come on,' he hissed, crossing the floor and through the doorway opposite.

The mice found themselves in a room drenched with gold. Gilt gleamed in delicate swirls, leaves, wreaths and bows, climbing up the walls to cherubs and the gleaming spokes of a vivid wheel on the ceiling. On the carpet sat gold chairs and tables, matching the drapes at the windows.

A swift glance around and questing sniffs assured the group that they were alone. Clocks ticked and suddenly chimed the hour – one o'clock. It was all Augustus needed to spur him on. He scurried in front of a huge marble fireplace and then paused before a chair backed up against the wall. His whiskers twitched. A current of air was coming from a cupboard next to the chair. It was a black cupboard with brightly painted panels but he could sense a gap behind it.

The little mouse carefully tiptoed up to the cupboard and sniffed the ground where it met the wall. There was definitely a gap and a strong whiff of human smells, too. It moved slightly when he pushed it – the door was not shut properly! Excitedly, he went to the end sticking out. He scrabbled and nudged and, at last, breathing in, he squeezed through the tiny gap he had made. Panting on the other side, he realized it was not a cupboard but a doorway. Augustus found himself on the landing of a short staircase – up or down? He turned back and squeaked to call the others through.

LOVE MISFIRES

The mice climbed up and found themselves in a passage with doors coming off at regular intervals. Augustus darted towards the first door. There was a generous gap at the bottom and they squeezed underneath. The room beyond was dark. Curtains drawn at the windows cut off most of the moonlight. In the dimness, they could make out the outlines of a sitting room. It was furnished in pale colours with brocade-covered seats, carved tables and images in gilt frames. A quick sniff around the room revealed another door.

'You see, I told you,' squeaked Drury. 'We'll be here forever!'

Augustus chittered, 'Drury, you and Lily wait here. No matter what happens, the two of you must wait here until we return. Is that clear? Gio, I want you to come with me through that door.'

Drury sighed and shrugged. Pushed to one side, as usual. On second thoughts his eyes brightened. This could be the luck he had been waiting for, a chance to work on his relationship with Lily. The setting was certainly romantic!

Left to their own devices, Drury and Lily spent a few minutes exploring the sitting room. Moonlight, escaping from the edges of the curtains, gave the room a soft glow. Plenty of hiding places, Drury noted gratefully. He always relaxed if he knew he could escape quickly when humans appeared.

Drury was so relieved he thought it might be a good moment to leave his scent with a pee. He sniffed cautiously along the huge polar bear fur lying in front of the fireplace. It seemed like a good place to do it. Then he reached the bear's snarling teeth and gleaming glass eyes. The little mouse froze. He swallowed hard. No, perhaps, *not*, he decided, backing slowly and carefully away.

Both mice scrambled up onto a sofa covered in brocade and lay on the edge of the seat. Lily became restless after a while and slowly paced along the satin cushions at the back. She seemed to enjoy the feel of the soft material caressing her side. Drury glanced back at her and grinned.

'Hey, have you tried this? Watch me!' Drury lay on his stomach, his front legs folded beneath him. He pushed forward with his back legs like a self-propelled toboggan, rubbing his belly against the cover of the seat.

'It's cool, you should try it,' he encouraged. His voice sounded a little croaky and caught in the middle as his throat hit a crease in the fabric.

Kneeling down with her front paws and using her back legs to push her, Lily wiped her face and chest along the cloth. She smiled at the feel of it against her skin. As she turned round to come back again, her nose touched Drury's coming in the other direction. She gasped, pulled back and sat up. Drury grinned.

'So, Drury . . .' she began, glancing quickly around to find a spot to settle. 'Tell me about yourself.'

Drury was taken aback for a moment. 'What do you want to know?'

'Oh, I don't know. Where you live, maybe? What's the food like? Do you have a big family? Things like that.'

Now that he had all Lily's attention, something he had been wanting ever since they started their journey, he found he was lost for words. Thinking rapidly, Drury knew he would need to edit some of his facts: his birth in an old pub, for instance, and his less-than-perfect progress through old Mother Snack's lessons. He remembered Lily's back roll on the carpet, the keen interest she had shown in all the rooms in the Palace, and her pleasure with the sofa tobogganing. It gave him a lead.

'Well,' he began uncertainly, 'I grew up in a place called the Royal Opera House. It's very like this place, actually.' Lily's eyes snapped wide open and she leaned forward to catch every word.

'I lived with my uncle because my father disappeared soon after I was born. My mother was poisoned just when

I was old enough to start learning the tricks of the trade.'
Lily nodded sadly. It happened.

'That really upset me; watching her slowly die, not knowing what to do, but . . .' Drury shrugged. 'I was young and had friends, cousins, my uncle, so it taught me to take life as it comes.'

Lily nodded again. 'So what are the humans like, there,' she prompted.

'They're okay, mostly. Humans come mainly to some parts of the building and not to others. Those parts are where the food is stored. Other parts have rows of seats and stairs like the ones we've been climbing, here. We have a curfew, too, but ours is at different times to yours. Humans visit my place when they want to rest together for a while in the dark. That's when we have our curfew.'

'Do your humans like us?' probed Lily curiously.

'No,' said Drury. He decided to change the subject. 'You asked about the food,' he offered brightly. 'It's amazing. The types of food keep changing and there's plenty of it, fish, omelette, salad, cake if you go for that sort of thing. If we want to try something different we can visit some of the eateries on the streets nearby. You'd love it!' Drury asked Lily about her food.

She shrugged. 'Oh, we have mostly crisps, or biscuit, chocolate maybe, or French fries and sometimes bits of sandwich or leftover burger. It's okay but I'd love to try something different.'

Drury's ears pricked up and he quivered. 'Why don't you come and visit sometime?' he suggested.

'What do you mean?' she asked softly.

'Well, when we've finished here I could show you round my place. It's near one of your stations – in running distance, anyway. The mice back home would be pleased to meet you.'

'Would they?' Lily sat up and gazed thoughtfully at the light-edged curtaining.

'Sure,' Drury sensed this was a delicate moment. 'I could take you to loads of interesting places too. Think about it,' he suggested.

'I will,' said Lily absently, 'I will.'

Drury smiled in the darkness. 'Eat your heart out, Knightsbridge,' he thought, feeling the warm glow of triumph.

'What's the story with Gio?' prodded Drury.

'What do you mean?'

'Well,' Drury shrugged, 'how long have you known him? How come the others all do what he says?'

'Oh, I see.' Lily thought for a moment. 'Gio's just become a messenger mouse,' she said proudly. 'Our Piccadilly messengers keep disappearing, so no one wanted to take on the role, but he volunteered. Messengers should be immune from attack, you see, because they share information with the whole system where we live. Information helps us all survive so that makes messengers special, like the forage captains.

'Anyway, I really got to know Gio when he became a messenger because he travelled through our station a lot. He stopped to play with the pups sometimes, if he wasn't in a hurry.'

''Okay, okay, I get the picture,' interrupted Drury. Pulling Lily away from Gio might be harder than he first thought. Still, he had done it before and if she preferred Gio, it would be more of a challenge! 'Wonder what's happened to the others,' he said.

'I can't even guess,' said Lily. 'I wonder what Merlin's secret is. It must be *very* important if he wants to give it to a human!'

DEAD END

While Lily and Drury were chatting, Augustus and Gio explored the room they had entered. It turned out to be a bedroom. The curtains at the window were not drawn and moonlight filtered in. Cut glass ornaments on an elegant dressing table cast rainbow splashes across the walls. In the pearly glow the intruders saw a large bed. It had a canopy curving above the pillows and sturdy posts on each side of the bed's brocade headboard. In its centre, moonlight glinted off gilt lettering that made Augustus gasp: EIIR.

Augustus slapped Gio with his tail. 'Gio,' he signed, 'this is the right place.'

Gio raised his eyebrows, 'yes?'

Augustus nodded. He was puzzled at the complete silence – there was no human breathing. 'The King should be up there,' he signed with his whiskers.

The mice scanned the area carefully, looking for a way to get onto the bed or to see the top of it. The bedside table was a possibility. Gio nudged the old mouse and pointed with his nose at the bedside drawers. The handles looked big enough to use as a ladder. Augustus shook his head.

He spied a chair with ornate carving and brocade covered seating. It stood beside the dressing table with the curtain draped behind it by the window. In front of the chair was a matching footstool. Augustus brightened. A jump from the stool to the chair seat would be manageable. The chair was a safe distance to see whether there was a man in the human nest.

'Let's try that,' he pointed with his nose.

Gio shrugged and followed him towards the window.

Augustus jumped onto the stool and waited to rest his back. He drew in his breath and leapt to the seat of the chair. Its fabric was slippery and he nearly slid back down to the stool. Quickly he gripped the material with his teeth and pulled himself forward. Gio watched Augustus's progress. When he could see that the old mouse was safely perched on the chair, he also jumped to the stool and then up to the chair. They peered at the bed.

To Augustus's dismay it was empty. He turned to Gio, eyes wide open in alarm, and said, 'nothing!'

Gio could see the old mouse was upset. He sniffed down Augustus's flanks with his nose to comfort him. 'Perhaps we have the wrong place,' he suggested gently.

'No,' shivered Augustus. 'How could we be wrong? This is where Merlin told me to come!'

Suddenly, a beating shadow rose up on the wall near the bed. Behind them came a loud tapping on the window. Both mice whirled around in fright. Sitting in the moonlight was a pigeon. It cocked its head on one side and gazed at them through the glass. Augustus stared at it and slowly approached the windowpane. He stood up and leaned his front paws against the glass. The bird lowered its beak to touch the glass within reach of the mouse's nose.

Gio had heard about birds but never seen one at close range. They seldom came to the bigger open-air Underground stations at night so did not meet station mice. The pigeon seemed enormous. It flapped its wings and started to tap the window. 'Watch out, Augustus,' he squeaked, 'it's going to attack!'

Augustus ignored him. Instead, he locked his beady eyes on the pigeon and put his head on one side as if listening. The bird tapped. It made a chuckling sound like throbble, throbble, and walked slowly to the edge of the windowsill. It stopped and bobbed its head back and forwards. Turning slightly towards the mice inside it cocked its head again while staring at Augustus. Slowly the bird marched to the end of the sill and sat down against the wall.

Augustus turned to Gio with a big smile. 'Excellent!' he said.

'Excellent?'

'Merlin has sent a message through this pigeon,' said Augustus. 'It seems the King does not sleep here, so we must return to the park. The pigeon tells me that Nutty will show us the way!'

ON TRACK

Augustus looked around the room where they had left the others, sniffing the air. He was anxious to move on.

Gio saw Lily and Drury safely sitting together on a brocade sofa. He frowned. 'Come on, you two, we've still got work to do!' Gio called up to them as he ran forward.

'Well, hello, to you, too, and thanks for taking your time,' piped up Drury. 'What took you so long?' he demanded.

'There's a problem,' said Gio. 'We've come to the wrong place.'

'*What*?' shrieked Drury. Lily gasped, her eyes wide with concern.

'Shut up, Drury,' hissed Gio. 'We don't want any dramatics from you!'

Drury screeched at Augustus. 'I thought you knew where we were going? You were positive this was the right place. You led us here without even hesitating that much!' he said. 'What happened in there? What now? We'll be trapped here, forever!'

Gio's patience snapped as he glared up at Drury. He said, with new authority in his voice, 'why don't you do everyone a favour, come down from there, and SHUT UP!'

Shocked silence quivered in the room.

'Yes,' sniffed Augustus, 'quite right, Gio! We must focus on what's important in a crisis. Now then, all we do is retrace our route in the Palace here, and return to the park. Instead of turning right we should have turned left. No harm done, only a bit of time lost.'

Lily jumped down and ran to Gio. She gave him a quick lick of support and turned to look up at Drury. 'Come on, Drury, let's go.'

With a loud sigh, Drury launched himself off the sofa and, on landing, shook his coat. 'Fine. Lead on, Mr Big Cheese,' he grumbled to himself, 'and excuse me for wanting to get a life, why don't you!'

Augustus was right: retracing their path through the Palace rooms was much quicker and easier than the mice expected. They could follow their own scent trail and were not so hesitant because now they knew the route. The mice raced across the Quadrangle outside. The moon had shifted in their absence but it still bathed the world in milky light. In the early hours of the morning the city slept. The mice passed the pillboxes and quickly crossed the forecourt, the gleaming road, and the cold, hard pavement. They were soon trotting into the edge of the tree-lined park.

Drury glanced back one last time to the dark lion statues on the golden mount. He gave everyone his opinion. 'Say what you like, Gussie, I'm not impressed with those humans!' He paused and shook himself as if shaking off an infection from the Palace. 'They're a bunch of cat worshippers! Did you see them all? Cat statues, cat images on the walls, cat feet on their furniture, cats prancing on the gates . . . cats everywhere! Dogs, too. Did anyone see a single mouse? Not one. It makes me mad!' The others ignored him.

It felt good to be out of the building and back on the move, but Augustus was nervous. Overcoming all the obstacles to get everyone to the Palace had taken a lot of energy, time and luck. It was most unlike Merlin to send him to the wrong place. And now, where was the help he had promised through the pigeon?

A squirrel slithered down a tree trunk and sat up in their path. 'Hello,' she said, 'are you Augustus?'

The old mouse stopped short and the others spread out beside him. 'Nutty?' asked Augustus.

'Yes, you're late. Follow me!' The grey squirrel bounded directly towards some buildings along the edge of the park.

'Wait,' shouted Augustus, "I can't keep up!'

The squirrel stopped to let the mice catch up. 'You really must hurry,' she complained. 'An owl's been hunting over the park recently. I don't want to be caught by him, thank you very much!'

Augustus shook his coat, sat up and sighed. A cool breeze stirred the dark mass of trees above, making the branches whistle eerily. It carried smells that told a bouquet of stories to those who knew how to make sense of them.

The old mouse lifted his nose for a quick check and then wished he had not. An unmistakable whiff was drifting on this current of air. Cat. There was even something familiar about this particular cat smell. Kaiser? Surely not! Could he, *would* he have followed them? Impossible! Perhaps it was a park cat. Was it . . . could the cat be . . . *stalking* them? The hair lifted down Augustus's back as he pondered. The smell was fairly fresh; the creature must be close by, or it passed by not long before.

'Do you smell what I smell?' he asked the others.

Lily's reaction was all the proof Augustus needed. He started trotting towards the squirrel with new energy. At a slower pace, they reached the roadway in front of the buildings and then veered to the right. Nutty safely led the mice along the base of a hedge. From time to time, Augustus paused and anxiously sniffed the air. He could not detect any cat smell or other dangers. So far, so good.

Coming to a pavement bordered by thin-hooped fencing, the squirrel stopped. To the left was a mighty gate across a tarred roadway. It was made of black railings, which looked familiar. They all sniffed the air for danger.

A few yards beyond the gateway on one side of the narrow road they noticed a sentry pillbox with a pointed roof. It was the same as those outside Buckingham Palace. In fact, further along was its twin. If this was the usual furniture of a palace entrance then they had found what they were looking for. The squirrel led them past into the road. She stopped opposite the black gate between the two pillboxes on guard.

'There you are,' said Nutty. 'What you seek is on the other side of that black gate . . .' and she bounded away like a grey ghost.

No humans were in sight, but the area was well lit by street lamps. The four mice trotted over the roadway to the dark barrier. Augustus was the last to wriggle under it. Before he did he tested the air with one final sniff and caught a whiff of something he recognized. There it was again: that smell from the park! This time the smell was fainter. If there *was* a cat on the prowl, the sooner they disappeared indoors, the better. Rather than scare the others, he kept his suspicions to himself. Following Drury he shimmied quickly under the gate.

GHOSTLY HELP

A carpet of speckled gravel stretched before the mice. It led towards a portico with four columns and a set of smooth curved steps on the left. The steps led up to a white double door. On each side of it an enormous oriental flowerpot stood to attention. The mice exchanged questioning glances. Once again, Gio led the way, making towards the door.

'What is this stuff,' chittered Drury, 'it's hurting my belly! Can't we find another way?'

The others ignored him, struggled on and eventually they all reached the steps. Coming to the doors, the mice found space along the bottom. If they breathed in and flattened down they could squeeze underneath. Behind the doors the place was silent.

They sat up, stroked their whiskers and gazed about them. Friendly moonlight filtered through glass panels set into the doors. It gave plenty of light to find their way. They were in a long narrow hallway, carpeted in red. A figured rug lay before them on the floor, with another beyond it. Along the sides of the hall were chairs and tables. Hanging on the walls were a vast tapestry and paintings. Overhead, a chandelier glinted with sparkling icicles. Fanning the air with their ears and whiskers revealed nothing, so the mice cautiously moved down the carpet. Gio led them towards the heavy wooden stairs he could see at the end of the hall.

Rooms opening off the hallway had their doors closed, but as they reached a statuette on a pedestal, a wide corridor opened opposite it on the right. The mice paused.

They could see a white marble staircase with elegant railings at the other end. In fact, the corridor looked just like passages in the Underground system with their posters on the walls. It seemed familiar and inviting. They turned towards it with relief and started trotting down the centre.

Drury trailed behind the others. He noticed, in passing, that the images were mostly of horses; even some of the ornaments on the bookcases were horses. He shook his head. It was when they were about half way down the corridor that Drury heard it: a menacing purr. He glanced back over his shoulder and froze.

'Um, Gio,' he quavered, 'look over here!'

The three mice trotting ahead of Drury stopped and turned around. He sounded badly shaken. There, silhouetted in the entrance to the corridor, was their old enemy. He was back again to haunt them: their worst nightmare, the vilest, cruellest danger in the world.

Drury's fur stood up; he could not move; he could hardly believe his eyes: Kaiser! Again! Where on earth had he come from? The purring grew louder and the cat's eyes gleamed. He licked his lips in excitement. Slowly, the cat padded, like a stalking lion towards his victims. His tail was fluffed and stiff with deadly intent.

'Quick, the curtains!' shrieked Drury, breaking the spell. He dashed to hide behind the floor-length drapes at the windows. Augustus did not hesitate. He dashed to the curtain further ahead and wriggled under its folds.

Lily dithered and then dived under the bench against the wall. Kaiser took after her with a snarl. Gio rushed to protect Lily. He chased the cat with a hiss and daredevil squeaks: anything to distract the animal from Lily.

Zigzagging around and then out from the sofa, Lily mesmerized Kaiser. She danced from side to side of the sofa leg like a swaying cobra. In frustration, Kaiser snatched out with his front paws but each time he missed – the leg got in the way!

Frustrated by Lily, the cat whirled to pounce on Gio instead, but he dodged away. Lily jumped to the top of the sofa then hissed and squeaked at Kaiser. The cat jumped up, but Lily dropped down and streaked under the seat.

Kaiser sprang from the sofa to pounce on Gio, but he missed again. Gio gave the cat a nip on the leg as he dashed out of reach.

The chase was on!

Gio drew Kaiser back along the corridor towards the hallway by sprinting against the wall. When he had lured Kaiser far enough, he shot back up the centre. As he rushed by, Kaiser stretched out and slashed Gio along his side with a claw. It off-balanced the mouse but he rolled over and staggered on.

'Gio!' shrieked Lily.

At that moment, help came from an unexpected quarter. A threatening growl came from the direction of the hallway statuette. It was a menacing rumble, a siren of death. Both mice and Kaiser paused and whirled to face the new danger.

Two corgis stood framed in the entrance to the corridor. Their lips were curled back in an ugly snarl. They bared long, sharp teeth and dark mouths. In the darkness they glowed with a blue-white light and their eyes gaped an empty black: ghosts from the past. Drury's eyes nearly popped from his head, he could barely breathe and felt faint.

The growling grew louder. The ghostly dogs advanced slowly towards the cat; their stumpy tails quivered in excitement. Kaiser's ears flattened, his tail drooped, his body tensed. He spat, whined and snarled at the dogs. They paused but did not stop growling. Then, as if at a shared signal, they attacked together.

Kaiser, with a terrified yowl and his tail high, ignored the mice and raced up the marble stairs at the end of the corridor. The dogs chased after him. In the distance, a young woman's voice called faintly, 'Bee, Billy, here boys, come here! Come on!' After a few moments, from the stairs came a sound of thumping, then the growl and screech of a cat in distress and, finally, ominously: silence.

The mice listened for a few minutes; then cautiously came out into the centre of the passage.

'Phew! Are you all right?' asked Drury, shakily crawling from his curtain hideout.

'Yes,' said Lily crossly, 'no thanks to you, though! A fat lot of help *you've* been!'

'I told you to head for the curtains!'

'Oh, thank you! If we knew what curtains were, that would be fine,' snapped Lily, warming up, 'but . . .'

'Calm down, Lily' warned Gio. 'We've still got to finish what we came for. We can't afford to squabble!'

Lily glared at Drury. 'Where's Augustus?' She squeaked as loud as she dared, 'Augustus!'

The old mouse poked his head out from under a curtain. 'Yes?' They all sighed with relief. 'What's happened to the cat?'

Lily ran over to him. 'We don't know but he's not here so you can come out. We must carry on.' Augustus crept slowly out and shook his coat. Lily turned to Gio and asked, 'are you hurt? I saw Kaiser strike at you. Let me check.'

The little mouse sniffed over Gio and assessed the scratch he'd received on his side. It did not seem to be serious – there was not much blood. Lily licked him over, 'there, that'll have to do.' Drury watched her with narrow eyes.

'Well done, everyone, but let's not forget why we're here,' said Augustus urgently. 'We must find out where the King is sleeping. Let's go back to where we were and carry on from there.'

PERSISTENCE WINS

After their brush with danger, the mice jumped up the stairs and moved cautiously against the wall. On the first floor they faced a copy of the wide carpeted hallway below but with different furnishings. Doors lined each side. On the left, a short way down was the entrance to another corridor.

'Now what?' signed Drury.

Augustus rounded on him. 'We set about finding the new King! He is close by but we have little time. I suggest you stop looking for problems, young Drury, and do your duty!' Augustus's outburst shocked the others.

'Why don't we give each room a sniff to start with,' said Gio quickly. 'Two tail slaps if you strike lucky,' he added.

They split up to give the space beneath each door a strong sniff. The corridor to the left smelled of Kaiser, so they gave it a wide berth. Augustus shook his head. We're not only hunting humans, he thought, we're also dodging a cat and dogs.

It was Lily who came across the first prospect. Sniffing along the bottom of a door she heard something move behind it. Excitedly, she slapped on the floor. The other mice came running.

Gio looked at Lily and Drury. 'Wait here. Come on,' he said to Augustus. The old mouse nodded and they both slid under the door.

Augustus took a few moments to get his bearings. He glanced despairingly at Gio, 'my back!' he signed. Gio pointed towards the bedside cupboard with his nose. It looked promising, especially as there was a pile of books on the floor next to it.

The younger mouse made a run for it. He galloped up to the books, jumped on top, leapt onto the side of the bed, swivelled, and shot across the small gap onto the top of the bedside cupboard. It took a few seconds. He needed a moment to catch his breath but then he leaned down to encourage Augustus.

The old mouse was grateful for the display but still not sure he could do the same thing. Not young enough, he decided.

Instead, he trotted towards the bottom of the bed where a robe was hanging to the floor. He found with a sniff that it was made of towelling. Augustus turned back, measured his distance and took a running jump up towards the top of the bed. He grasped the robe with his teeth and used his paws and his mouth to climb the short distance to the top.

After catching his breath, the old mouse trudged between the edge of the bed and the lumpy human shape sleeping peacefully beside him. When he reached the pillow he jumped across to Gio waiting on the bedside table.

Both mice sat up and peered anxiously at the face of the person sleeping in front of them. The human was lying down the middle of the bed on her back. Augustus could not recognize the face before him. What a dilemma! He sniffed and his nose took him back to flowers and the sweet aura of the countryside. The human had longer hair than he expected and the shape of the face was not the same. He turned gloomily to Gio and shook his head.

'Wrong one,' he whiskered silently. 'This is a female'.

Gio's shoulders sagged as he groomed his whiskers and nibbled at his paws. 'We'll have to keep looking,' he signed to Augustus. Gio leapt across the gap to the bed, flopped down to the pile of books beside it, and jumped to the floor. With Augustus behind, he scurried over to the door and squeezed underneath.

Lily was waiting patiently for them on the other side. She lay with her tail curled forward, her chin resting lightly on the tip. There was no sign of Drury. 'Okay, where is he?' hissed Gio.

'Don't be angry,' said Lily calmly. 'He went to check the rest of the rooms to see if there were any more with humans in them.'

Augustus sat up and started grooming his whiskers thoughtfully.

'Oh that's great! That's just wonderful!' muttered Gio and started pacing up and down beside Lily. She watched him anxiously.

'We only have a cat, plus two savage monsters roaming around in this place; not to mention a bunch of humans behind some of these doors! Did I mention an ancient sorcerer getting his directions wrong? I mean, pleeeese . . . I had nothing else to do, did I? There I was bored out of my mind, going crazy with nothing to do! The most dangerous thing to happen right now is for us to split up. I told you both to *wait here*. This is stupid, stupid, time-wasting.' Gio sat down and groomed his whiskers. He was quivering all over with stress.

Before his companions could do anything Drury interrupted them.

'Hey, what's up?' came his cheery squeak, 'what's stupid?'

Lily sat up quickly. 'Don't ask!' she replied. Gio pursed his lips, closed his eyes for a moment and breathed very deeply. Augustus peered at Drury intently.

'Guess, what?' Drury darted to them across the carpet.

'*What*?' Gio snapped.

'What's the matter with *you*?' asked Drury, taken aback.

'Never mind,' signed Lily, 'just tell us.'

Drury shrugged. 'I found another room with a human inside. It's just down here.'

Gio's body sagged with relief. 'Good,' he said. 'Show us the way!'

Drury proudly led the way back across the carpet to a door near the end of the hall. His ears flicked towards the gap under the door. 'After you maestros,' he said with a flourish of his tail.

'No. You and Lily wait here as before,' said Gio. 'Watch out for Kaiser and, if he comes, head him off.'

Gio and Augustus wriggled under the door again. They paused to check the room before them. As in Buckingham Palace, there was a large bed against the opposite wall. Augustus noticed the image of three feathers carved discreetly into the headboard of the bedstead. His ears pricked up.

The listening mice could hear regular human breathing. A robe was lying where it had been thrown across the bottom of the bed. Gio streaked across the carpet towards it. He leapt as high as he could and, pulling on the robe's fabric with his mouth and claws, he scrambled up.

Augustus followed as nimbly as he could. Gio led the way along the human body towards its head. As they neared the pillows the human moved!

MERLIN

The mice froze. The human turned over to face the bedside and pulled his blanket up. Tumbling over, the mice grabbed the heaving surface beneath them with their teeth and claws. When the quake settled they found themselves at the edge of the mattress.

Augustus felt the blood pounding in his ears. He could not believe it. For one heart-stopping second he wanted to be somewhere, anywhere, *else*. He would have given anything to whiz back home and go to sleep. His nerves were starting to snap with the tension of the night. He closed his eyes and opened them. He was still stuck, on a bed with a sleeping human. The man's breathing settled into a rhythm.

Gio stretched up to peep over a fold in the blanket. Ahead of him was Augustus crouched in a tiny lump shuddering with fright. A short cupboard sat next to the side of the bed near the pillows. The clutter on top could be used for hiding. Gio took a deep breath and crept lightly forward to the old mouse. Augustus squeaked and jumped when Gio stretched forward and licked his side. Gio sniffed the old mouse along his flanks to reassure him. 'Okay?' he signed with a smile.

Augustus sighed deeply and sank to lay his head on his front paws. Gio let him rest for a moment and nudged his shoulder. He pointed towards the top of the bedside cupboard with his nose. Augustus slowly picked himself up and padded forward stiffly. He gathered himself and sprang over the gap to land on top of the cupboard. Gio followed. They took cover under a framed photograph of two young humans that stood beside them. Again they paused and listened, whiskers quivering. All seemed well.

From this view point Augustus peered across at the face lying on the pillow opposite. This time there was no mistake: it was the face Merlin had shown him on the rock! It was The King. A thrill of triumph shot through him. Merlin *was* helping, after all!

Augustus sat and raised his paws like a Medicine Man before an Indian tepee. He swallowed and firmly declaimed the spell Merlin had given him. He swayed his body; paws stretched out and murmured the incantation. Its poetic words soothed his anxious heart.

Crouched beside him, Gio lay down resting his head on his front paws. He watched Augustus sway gently from side to side. His eyelids drooped; the soothing murmur of the old mouse relaxed him. Augustus's voice crooned his spell, driving its mysterious words into the dreams of the man before him.

In seconds they were drifting . . . drifting in a dark swirl of smoky air that carried a trace of wood smoke. Augustus tried to wake up. He knew it was important to wake up but it was difficult because he felt so tired. The little mouse forced his eyes open. It was dark except for a few flickering points of golden light. Slowly the dimness took shape.

There was light on the floor against a wall. It jumped up and down in yellows, oranges and reds, like a living thing. It let a swirl of wispy smoke escape. The smoke turned darker as it rose up, bumped against the roof, curled black and crept out to an opening. Augustus recognized it. 'Fire' the humans called it – and they feared it, as mice did. The spell had brought them to Merlin's holy place.

Reflections from the fire danced on walls of stone. They played with glass of different colours or metals of silver and brass. Plants, driftwood, crystals and books sat on shelves in a medley of shapes and shadows. A patchwork curtain of animal skins was drawn across the opening to the cave, making it warmer and cosier. Three lamps with low flames shed a dim light in the back of the cave.

A big shadow moved in front of Augustus and threw a log onto the fire. It hissed and spat throwing sparks into the air. The dark shape was a human. Wrapped in a grey, hooded cloak, he sat on a Roman chair, leaning on one arm to watch the flames. Here was a human who *controlled* the thing called 'fire' and made it serve him! Augustus felt a thrill of pride that he served such a powerful master. He felt the tickle of soft fur against his back. He drew away to find out what it was. To his horror, he was tucked into the belly of a wolf cub! His squeak of fright roused the old sorcerer. The little mouse sprinted towards Merlin to hide beneath his robe. The magician caught him by the tail and stood up.

'Ah ha!' he exclaimed, 'visitors to my humble cave.' Holding Augustus before him, the man turned him around, recognized something and chuckled. 'My Caesar, I salute thee!'

Gio crouched quivering when the human, rising as a black looming shadow, came towards him. The man bent down and, like a striking snake, he grabbed Gio's tail: plucking him into the air to dangle in front of his face. 'But what is this? I know thee not. Who art thou?' Gio squeezed his eyes shut as the man turned him around, inspecting him.

Augustus chittered rapidly to the man, who returned to his seat by the fire. Placing both mice gently down on each knee, he rubbed his hands together. 'It works, it works,' he announced to the creatures resting near the fire: a badger, a greyhound and a squirrel. Above them Augustus could see a roosting pigeon on a shelf and an owl on a perch. The wolf cub slapped its tail on the ground in a half-hearted wag and raised its head to look at Merlin.

Augustus faced the man and sat up. 'Sire, I have obeyed thy message. I am with the spirit of the monarch as thee foretold.'

'Aye, my virtuous servant, thou hast the right of it. Our royal spirit has travelled with thee!'

Merlin gently carried both mice to a table at the back of his cave. He returned to the wolf cub. It had the round tubbiness of a puppy and thick fluffy fur. Opening his arms in welcome he bowed and said, 'my greetings, Sire. A humble audience, I beg, that I may share the secrets of power over this fair and worthy land? Rest now, if it please thee, for I have much to tell, but it is for trusted ears alone.'

MERLIN HONOURS THE KING

Once the wolf cub had settled itself before the fire, Merlin went back to the waiting mice. They cowered down before the dark hooded mass that blocked the firelight. 'Who is this with thee?' Merlin asked Augustus roughly. 'Do ye bring a noble mouse, pure in heart and of a good mind? Is he to be trusted? Or is it a villain that has followed thee? His presence here has put his mortal soul in danger. Why is he here?'

Gio gazed up at the hooded man that spoke the language of mice and cocked his head. The man noticed his gesture. He half smiled.

'Sire,' faltered Augustus anxiously, 'my family has perished and I am old; I needed help to do thy bidding. This mouse is my faithful guide and supporter. He was present when I brought the King to thee. He has heard thy special call. The fault is mine. Protect him from thy curse, I beg of thee!' Augustus pleaded. 'He is a worthy mouse and true to thy cause. He is a messenger for the mice in London and will have need of thy care.'

The man was silent for some minutes pondering the fire then he drew back his hood and revealed his face. It was old and weathered, with a beak of a nose, thick grey eyebrows, a wide, firm mouth and slate grey eyes. His head was topped with white hair, cut short but ragged, and he had a badly trimmed white beard.

'What is thy name?' Merlin asked Gio sternly. His eyes seemed to pierce Gio's heart.

'G-Gio, Sire, Giorgio Knightsbridge,' he croaked.

'Giorgio, it is, then!'

When the man smiled, Augustus relaxed. He had hoped Merlin would like Gio and he wanted to create a bond between them. This was the man who linked the human and natural worlds, blending them in harmony. His living spirit balanced their energies. 'Sire, I have sensed division and unrest among the mice in London. Here, thou hast a young and dedicated mouse that can champion thy cause and keep faith in thy purpose.'

Frowning the old sorcerer slowly twisted the ring on his forefinger. 'It is impossible to remove the curse and a price will be paid for this transgression, Augustus. But I shall do what I can to deflect its power; for, verily, it is brave to challenge the Fates! I shall mark this mouse that all may know he is my servant. That will protect him. Then we shall see . . .'

Merlin went to fetch a small pot from a chest, which he placed on the table. He put an oil lamp in its centre and took off his ring. Lifting a thong from his neck, he slipped onto the table its turquoise and amber beads, snake fangs and bear claws then threaded it through the ring. This he held over the flame for a few minutes. Both mice watched his activities with interest. Merlin laid the ring gently on the table and released it from the thong. Using the cloth at the end of his sleeve, he carefully picked up the hoop of the ring. He turned Gio onto his side and held him firmly then applied the face of the ring to his haunch, saying:

'I make this mark,
Within its ring,
For one who's life
Now serves a King.'

Augustus remembered the pain and the smell of burned hide. He suffered a pang of guilt when he heard Gio squeal and saw him wriggle. The old sorcerer chuckled. Next, he opened the pot he had brought and dabbed a greasy ointment on Gio's burn. It soothed the mouse's skin immediately. Gio tried to lick his wound but it tasted vile so he left it alone. Augustus sniffed gently down Gio's side and sat beside him grooming his whiskers to comfort the stricken mouse.

For a moment Merlin's expression softened. He stretched out a finger to stroke their backs then he put back the pot in his chest. 'Now we are bound in eternal trust,' he said. 'Living creatures revere Merlin. Some think I am a god but, nay, 'tis not true; 'tis only a sign of respect or perhaps fear!'

Merlin strode over to the patch-skin curtain, which he pulled aside. 'Away, my friends! My gift and my blessing are for the King and not for thee. I will recall thee when it is time. He will have much to ponder.'

On his command, the animals and birds dozing in his cave, woke up, stretched or ruffled their feathers, and went out into the starlit night beyond his cave. He came to the table where Augustus and Gio were waiting.

'I have something to show thee, my faithful Augustus.'

Merlin turned to one side and clapped his hands in a signal. From the back of the cave a group of mice came running towards him: some pure white, others brown or grey and some jet-black. They settled about his feet and waited. Merlin peered intently as if searching for one particular mouse. He saw it. Reaching out, he grabbed it by the tail, and placed it gently on the table.

Gio and Augustus looked at the mouse and then Augustus cried out, 'Tia!' Both mice squeaked a greeting and rushed to sniff flanks and tickle whiskers. Merlin watched, with a sad smile, Gio in embarrassed silence.

The old sorcerer explained, 'thy daughter did her duty, Augustus! She took the secret of kingship to her Queen. And, see: she did not die but lives on in spirit. Again, I fulfilled my promise to my people. My energy is tiring and the time link will soon be closing.'

Merlin added the three mice to the group on the floor at his feet. He led them all to the mouth of the cave where he pulled aside the curtain. As Gio passed by, Merlin picked him up and gently put him down on a flat rock at the entrance, which he used as a seat.

'Fear not the owl, for he has marked thee as my messenger and will not harm thee,' murmured Merlin.

The sorcerer turned back into his cave and let the curtain fall.

DUTY DONE

Merlin's servants were left to themselves. Gio sat up, gazed at the moon and sniffed strange night scents on the air. Augustus and his daughter scampered away. The other creatures from Merlin's cave had not wandered far. They scattered under the trees and bushes that ringed its approach, waiting patiently for their master.

'Tia, what happened to you? Why did you not return?'

'Oh, Papa, a mouse in the Underground helped me take the spirit of the human Queen to Merlin. When I was ready to return he asked me to stay with him as his mate. I loved him. I was on my way to tell you when another mouse caught me. He was jealous. He asked me to stay with him but I refused. He was so enraged he killed me so that I could not go back to you or to my beloved. He is evil. He means to cause havoc because he wants control. There are bad times to come.'

Augustus was aghast. 'Who is this mouse?'

'They will soon find out, he is nearly ready to show his ambition.'

A loud rhythmic clapping snapped across the night air. Merlin was finished with the wolf cub and summoning the other creatures back. He came out to pick up the visiting mice by the tail and take them into the cave.

'No time to lose, my good fellows,' said the sorcerer cheerfully. 'Time to return, for ye have important work to do for me.'

Not all the inhabitants of the cave came back to watch the visitors depart. Merlin's other assistants would return in their own time. He closed the skin curtain to cut off draughts. The wolf cub was lying down on his stomach. His front legs were stretched out towards the fire, his eyes blinking sleepily as they looked into the flames. Merlin laid the mice gently down by the side of the cub, and then sat on his own chair.

'Sire,' ventured Augustus, 'I beg one question before we go. The secret of kingship given to men . . . can ye give it also to mice? We, too, have need of a great leader.'

The sorcerer smiled. 'Tell me what maketh a great leader?'

Augustus swallowed. 'I know not, Sire. Wisdom?'

Merlin turned to Gio. 'And thee? What must a leader be to inspire thee to follow?'

Gio blinked. 'Brave?'

Merlin sighed. 'If I asked each of my servants, the answer would be different. The qualities for great kingship change over time, their kingdoms evolve and the nature of their challenge is never the same. There is a new proving for each King and likewise for their people. The world of men is not that of mice, just as the world of deer is not that of fish!

'Nay, the secret comes from the Song of Old and can have no meaning for thee. It links with the rhythms of Time and of the heavens. It is unique, crafted to blend the monarch with the nation's destiny. As our nation grows, therefore the guidance adapts to meet what is to come. This is not for mice, Augustus. Thy world hath its own destiny. Have faith in my care and all will be well.'

Merlin leaned forward and took a smoking twig from the fire. He waved the twig slowly in the air in front of the visiting animals. It smelled fragrant, herbal. The cave, and Merlin, became dim until they were peering into darkness. A great void crept through them: the cold gloom of loss and the sadness of goodbye. Augustus felt himself falling asleep. He tried to fight against it – but to no avail. He soon dozed off . . .

ESCAPE

When Augustus slipped out of his trance, he did not know where he was. Looking around, he found himself lying under a photograph tepee. Then he remembered what had happened. Gio was lying on his side, his whiskers askew. Augustus was worried about the return journey. After all the excitement they had gone through, would he be able to cope. The Underground mice could help him through their terrain but after that . . . With a shrug, Augustus waited. All he could hear was the sound of regular breathing from the bed. He judged it safe to move.

The little mouse rose, stretched, and nudged Gio to wake him. Gio slowly rolled onto his belly and shook his head. Like Augustus he blinked hard and looked about him. Finally, he got up and sniffed a few steps over to the edge of the bedside table.

Augustus jumped across to the back of the pillows in front of him. When Gio followed suit, he skirted carefully around the resting head and scurried down to the foot of the bed. Reaching the robe, he slithered quickly down its folds to the floor. Gio arrived with a thump beside him. After shaking his coat Gio followed his own scent back to the door. Augustus ambled slowly behind him. Squeezing under it, they found Lily and Drury waiting.

'And about time, too!' Drury signed quietly. 'What do you make of *that*?' He nodded towards the stairs.

Sitting primly with his back to the mice, his ears pricked forward, gazing intently between the banister rails, was a glowing blue corgi!

Augustus's heart kicked in alarm. They had to leave but how were they to get past the animal? Glancing around desperately, Augustus remembered the corridor they had passed on their way to the bedrooms. It gaped invitingly between them and the dog's back. 'Come along!' he signed and darted forward, keeping to the skirting board along the wall and lifting up his tail.

The others edged around the base of a bureau and dashed under a table, all the time getting nearer and nearer to the ghostly hound guarding the staircase. As they reached the open corridor on their right, the dog lay down, stretching along the top step. There was still some distance between them but the mice jerked to a halt. Their hearts thumped, as they waited for him to settle. The dog's ear twitched back for a second and then flicked forward again.

Taking a chance, Augustus scuttled away. The carpeting masked any sound of their passage. As soon as they judged it to be safe, the mice pelted as fast as their nimble paws could carry them. They rushed along the wide corridor to the marble stairs at the end. It was when they drew close to the top step that Gio stopped suddenly.

'What is it?' asked Lily panting.

'Smell!' snapped Gio.

'The others sniffed the air and picked up Gio's alarm. There could be no mistaking it – CAT. This was the staircase Kaiser had used to escape from the corgis. But the smell was stale.

'Come on,' chivvied the old mouse, 'we need to get out of here.'

The four of them cautiously moved over to the stairs. Their ears and noses worked furiously seeking danger. At the top they peered down the pale marble stairwell. It was much darker at this end of the house with no windows opening onto the steps. They flopped down to the floor below.

At the bottom, Augustus noted all the horse images and the furniture. Framed in the opening at the other end was a statuette he recognised. The long corridor stretching away on the right was the same place they had confronted Kaiser! They were on the right track.

'This way,' he said. The mice sprinted along the figured rugs up the passage. Reaching the end, they checked for danger. To the left, the air seemed fresher and the hallway was lighter. Moonlight streamed in through the glass panes across the door at the end. There it was: the gateway to safety. They all veered down the hall towards it.

Drury and Lily reached the door first and wriggled frantically through the thin gap beneath. Augustus was heavier and tired. He scrabbled with his paws and at one stage seemed to be stuck. Gio pushed his rump to help.

Suddenly, behind them a loud yap announced the arrival of the second dog. It stood with one paw up, frozen by the sight of two mice where there should be nothing at all. Seeing them get away, it yelped for help and charged towards them. Gio glanced over his shoulder at the looming threat. Long white teeth, black wicked eyes, large dark ears and menacing growls thundered towards him.

'Merlin help us,' he shrieked. He scrambled under the barrier, his tail whipped through in the nick of time.

A noisy thump rattled the bolt holding the centre of the doors to the floor. The mice could hear paws scrabbling on the other side of the door accompanied by frustrated yelps and snuffling. The door held firm. Augustus jumped hastily off the front doorstep. Without a backward glance he rushed after the others. Down the entrance steps he charged, across the gravel, straight for the black gate to the roadway. They had done it. They were out! Now for the home run . . .

Outside the gate the night was quiet. Moonlight gleamed on the surface of the roadway.

'We'd better be careful,' warned Lily, looking around her with a shiver. 'If it's not cats, it's dogs; if it's not dogs, it's humans. We need to hide.'

The mice moved as one to wait by the dark pillbox next to the gatepost.

'Uh oh,' murmured Drury. 'I'm picking up a bad smell. Is it just me or do you smell it, too?'

Augustus sniffed the air and the hair down his back rose. Fresh cat smells were drifting towards them on a faint stir of breeze coming from the right. It was the same smell he had sniffed on their way in.

'That does it,' said Gio with a questioning glance at Lily. 'What do you think? Kaiser?'

She nodded miserably. 'The one-and-only!'

Gio grinned to cheer her up. 'Makes it an easy decision – let's go the other way. Thanks for the help, Kaiser – so kind of you!' Lily giggled.

'Are you alright, Augustus?' Gio asked. 'Do you want to rest? If so, we'll need to find somewhere safe.'

The old mouse sighed. Merlin's spell had made him very thirsty. 'I need a drink.'

'Of course,' said Gio, 'come on, we must look for it.' Taking the lead, he darted across the road and retraced their trail towards the black barred gate. Jumping through, they pattered slowly along the base of the hedge until it ended at the bottom of the tarred roadway. Beyond was a welcoming sight. The vast stretch of grass carpeting the ground under tall trees looked familiar. It beckoned.

'This is the park where we met Nutty!' said Augustus.

Gio nodded. 'Across this open patch is the signpost.' The mice sprinted along their own scents until they noticed something away to their left. It was the giant gateway from before and beyond it: the golden mount. They were on the right track . . .

IN MEMORIAM

The gurgle of falling water carried faintly on the air. Gio lifted his nose and sniffed. He squeaked to call the others. 'I'm sure that's water!' he told them when they arrived. 'It must be close, you can hear it.'

The mice fanned out and advanced over a gentle mound of turf drawn by the magnetic trickle of running water. They came upon some rough cobblestones, set in place by men. Encouraged by this evidence, they slipped and slithered over them and came to a smooth flat surface with strange markings patterning the edge. The circle of stone was laid bare to the sky. Different coloured marble radiated out from a metal circle in the centre. A fringe of dark metal lettering was stamped into the outer rim. The space was a useful platform to regroup.

'I wonder what this is,' said Lily, sniffing around her curiously.

Gio shrugged and said, 'who knows? Probably another kind of human sign.'

'Yes!' Drury exclaimed in a ghoulish voice. 'It's a sacrifice stone where their chief kills a special mouse every year to bring the human tribe good fortune! Raaaaar!'

Augustus interrupted, 'it's a memorial stone. Humans use it to remind them to grieve. If we're going to have a drink we must hurry and keep moving. We haven't the time to waste.'

Ahead of the mice stretched a short path of the same cobblestones and then they could make out a strange monument. It rose up in a slight gradient to point at the starry sky. The sound of running water was coming from that direction. They hesitated a moment to check for danger then scurried towards the water.

The mice arrived at the base of three steps shaped like a wide V. Now that they were closer to the big edifice it became clearer. It was designed like a flat square laid on the ground with one corner pushed down so that the opposite corner stuck up into the air. Water ran down the flat surface from the raised point at the top. It rippled over some maple leaves trapped on its face and disappeared through a grill tucked under the bottom step. The water smelled fresh and very inviting.

Dead leaves, caught against the grill blocked the water, forming a small pool. Gio jumped down the steps, and ran towards it. The others followed. The flat surface of the fountain made it easy to reach the water and drink. It was bliss. Gio let the cold water gently sooth the burn in his side.

When they had drunk their fill, Drury started to play about. He jumped beyond the trapped water onto the flat marble surface. He splashed Lily and waded up to Augustus in a sploshy rush. Lily giggled and pulled back to keep her coat dry. Then Drury discovered that the maple leaves were made of metal set into the marble. When he knocked against one it bruised him. He squeaked loudly and made a fuss staggering around it.

The mice were making a lot of noise but it cheered them up. Augustus did not have the heart to stop them – they needed a bit of fun. As he was shaking droplets of water from his coat, a dark shadow passed over them. He looked up, suddenly uneasy. They were clearly exposed in the moonlight. All his anxieties about this alien place came flooding back.

'Come on,' he called. 'Time to go.'

'Killjoy!' muttered Drury under his breath. But he made his way to the edge of the water chute and leapt out.

As the mice shook the water from their hides, a dark shadow again passed overhead and Augustus suddenly felt afraid: afraid as he never had before. 'Run!' he shouted urgently.

Stumbling up the steps and along the cobbled surface to the flat stone he led them towards the trees nearby. Augustus's fear quickly passed to the others. They soon overtook him as they raced for shelter.

The air around the mice became agitated. A whispering sound chased them from behind. They reached the flat marked stone but, as they rushed across its face, soft feathers brushed over their backs. Bowled over by the owl they picked themselves up and continued to run in frenzy. They were fast, but not fast enough. Then it happened: a dreadful mousy scream wailed behind them. Their hearts thumped, blood rushed in their ears. A series of shrieks passed over their heads, rising up into the air. High above, the squeaking cut off as they reached a pathway under the trees.

Augustus had gone!

Under the canopy of branches the terrified mice shot up the slope of the park. The owl's brutal snatch made them run like wind in a train tunnel, but they could not keep it up. Exhaustion brought the mice to a halt. Panting heavily, they staggered about in circles to catch their breath.

A kindly witness peered down at them from a branch. Her bushy tail was kinked up behind her and her big dark eyes watched intently. It was a dangerous night. Old Tawny was out hunting and so was the cat that had just passed by. The squirrel shivered. Cats climbed trees: she had seen it. Nutty's eyelids drooped as she dozed off to sleep.

Gio gazed at the fading stars. 'I've got the strangest feeling!' He turned to Lily. 'I think that was Merlin's owl!'

Lily's mouth opened, '*what*?'

Gio stared at Lily and Drury. 'That was Merlin's owl. I'm sure of it. He's taken Augustus to be with him. Augustus is home at last with his daughter and with Merlin.'

'Oh, I do hope so!' said Lily.

Gio nodded and smiled, 'I think he was dreading going back to the country. He must have been lonely there. Come on, we need to get back home ourselves.'

CHEERS . . .

The three mice trudged slowly up the slope to Green Park station. At the park gates they hesitated. They sniffed the air, looking confused. Drury ended the moment. 'I suppose this is where I say goodbye?' He threw Gio a challenging stare, 'because I'm not going back down there and that's final.'

Gio sat up and gave Drury a long measuring look. He nodded. 'In that case, it is goodbye.' With a half smile he added, 'and good luck with the cats!'

Drury seemed surprised. He looked at Lily and back at Gio. 'What . . . you're letting me go? No argument? Just like that?' and he smacked his tail on the pavement. 'You're going to leave me here and go back down there? Why don't you stay up here?'

'It's our home, Drury. There are problems down there but they're not *your* problems.' Gio paused. 'I understand that. You would have left Augustus and his mission with a wink and a flicked whisker. I'm a Merlin mouse now and I have work to do. For what it's worth – although you were a pain at times, I'm glad you came along.'

Drury raised an eyebrow. 'Wow! Now he tells me!'

'You were there – in case,' said Gio.

Drury nodded. Leadership was not his thing, but survival was.

'Cheerio, then,' Gio twirled his whiskers and twitched his nose in a casual mouse salute. He turned and without a backward glance, darted along the pavement towards the stairs leading down to Green Park station.

Drury turned to Lily. 'Come with me,' he pleaded. 'I can show you lots of things . . .' he started. She shook her head. 'I can take you to exciting places, you'll meet some great characters, eat exotic food, believe me, we'll have fun!'

'Drury, stop!' she exclaimed. 'I don't want to stay with you. That's my home! What you've told me is not enough. Sure, we have problems down there but I need to be with my mice now, when they need me. What kind of mouse do you think I am that I'd leave my friends and little orphans? I'm sorry; I have to go. Why don't *you* join *us*?'

Drury snorted dismissively and shook his head. 'This is my world up here – air that's clean, plenty of food, freedom to roam wherever you want. I can't live down there. Why don't you stay here and be my mate-for-life?'

Lily's mouth dropped open. '*Me*?'

Then, a smile tugged at the corner of her mouth. 'Oh, no,' she chittered softly, 'you see, there's someone else.'

Lily's eyes twinkled at the expression on Drury's face. 'I lost my heart to him some time ago. We've just been so busy I haven't done anything about it yet. Don't worry, I'm working on it!' Lily shrugged as she explained further, 'Gio needs me, you see. You don't need anyone.'

Drury's mouth crumpled. He had hoped . . . 'I understand.' He thought for a moment and then quickly, before Lily could duck away, his nose touched hers. He grinned.

'Goodbye, hope all goes well down there,' he said brightly.

Lily blinked rapidly, turned and ran. Gio would be waiting.

Left alone on the pavement, Drury noticed the light was getting stronger. A half-hearted dawn was creeping over the city. There had been many losses already in his life. Goodbyes always hurt and they never got easier to bear.

A van hummed past him belching exhaust fumes. It roused him from a dream about the might-have-been. The current of air billowing after it brought some promising smells. They seemed to be coming from a yellow rubbish tip on the opposite side of the street. His stomach gurgled. The rubbish might be worth investigating.

Trotting to the edge of the pavement, he paused to check for danger before crossing the road. As he started towards the huge container, a movement caught his eye. Drury froze. Coming out of it was a dark, furry head with green eyes, whiskers and pricked up ears. A lithe mottled body with a fluffed up tail followed it. The cat teetered on the edge of the container and then jumped to the ground. As it moved away, Drury could see it was limping. There was no mistaking that creature – Kaiser! The rubbish could wait.

Drury reversed smartly and ran to the shelter of the park wall. He glanced back across the street and saw Kaiser padding slowly into an entrance. Hanging above it was a red and blue sign that said: UNDERGROUND. Relieved, Drury remained where he was to re-plan.

Bright white lights stretching across the pavement some way to his right caught his attention. He stared hard at the lettering, but could not make sense of it. The size and condition of the building seemed promising, though. Also, it was on the same side of the road.

'Might as well start there as anywhere,' Drury muttered to himself. 'Looks the kind of place where there could be good pickings. Think I'll take a chance on it.'

As there were no threats in sight, the survivor sauntered along Piccadilly and entered his new home under the front door. The lights above it said:

THE RITZ

Although Penny was born in the Far East, she grew up in Africa. Her parents moved a lot because of her father's work and she found the disruption difficult. After university she taught French in secondary schools abroad for 5 years. She moved to the UK in the early 1980s and loved its cheerful zest for life.

Although working mostly in the education sector – teaching, secretarial, developing policy or qualifications – Penny has also worked in hospitals and in retail.

During a life of continual change and upheaval, Penny found reading a comfort, an inspiration and an escape. It is a skill that keeps on giving . . .

www.ingramcontent.com/pod-product-compliance
Lightning Source LLC
Chambersburg PA
CBHW051810050726
47598CB00006B/2493